The
LUCKY
Machine
AIMÉE COZZA

Illustrations & book cover by Aimee Cozza

Edited by Amanda Silva

First edition 2025

ISBN: 979-8-9915214-3-7 (paperback)
979-8-9915214-4-4 (hardcover)
979-8-9915214-5-1 (ebook)

Author's website: aimeecozza.com

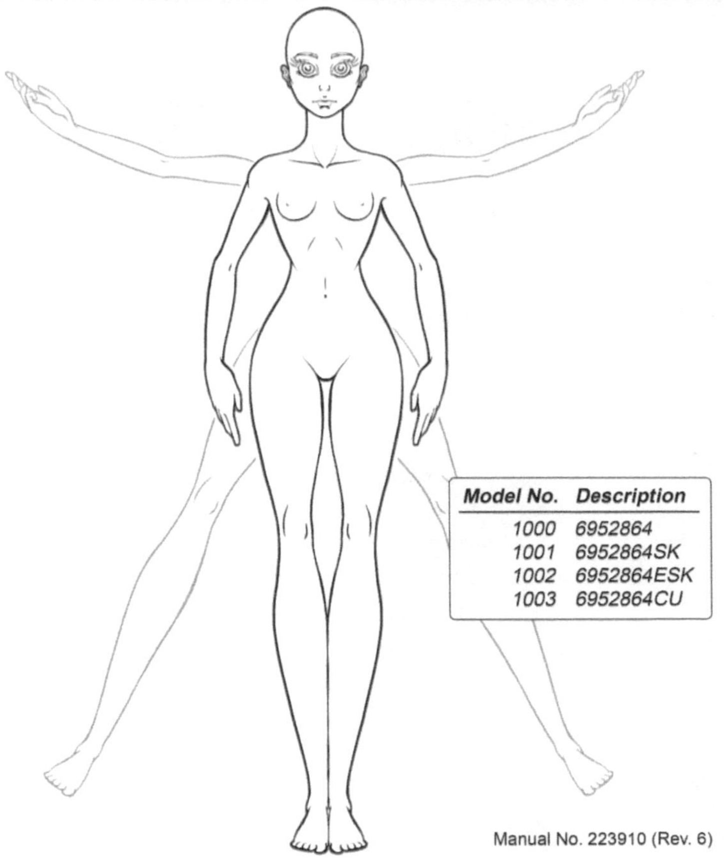

Model No.	Description
1000	6952864
1001	6952864SK
1002	6952864ESK
1003	6952864CU

Manual No. 223910 (Rev. 6)

CONTENT AND TRIGGER TOPICS

This book is a work of pure fiction and focuses on the struggles of a select few robots. These robots have a different way of navigating and experiencing the world. However, many of the themes in this book may be metaphors or adjacent to sensitive topics.

Death
Violence
Dubious consent scenarios
Sex work and sex slavery
Racism
Slavery and indentured servitude
Anxiety and anxiety attacks
Suicide and attempted suicide
Loss of limb

00110001: 1

Falling was the first memory of her new life that didn't exist solely in data glitches, trace apparitions, and hallucinations.

The first memory she got to keep.

It was equal parts joyous and terrifying; the simple albeit custom skinned NX personal model android knew what joy was from the day she was initialized, though it had taken some time out of her box to learn about fear. As a personal android, she was not well equipped to know what to do *after* she had jumped, and she had mere microcycles to process such an eventuality, but she had made the tiny movements necessary to cause her body, laid across the rail for cleaning, to slide into the spaces towards the lower levels. It had taken surprisingly little to slip, just a slight movement in one of her actuators.

Maybe she would fall forever. She did not know how many levels carried the city *down*, exactly, and where it may have stopped, if it even *did* stop. She just knew that the uncertainty of down was better than anything above.

At least, better than anything she knew about above.

The NX had jumped.

Her programming, keening rampant with the decision — perhaps the first *real* decision she had ever made for herself — was struggling to compensate, locking up her system, at least partially.

She had no way to expect the impact which was in fact not an impact at all. Her proximity sensors would have alerted her to an incoming floor, a rail, a sign, a wire, but her system seemed frozen, and even if it hadn't been, she couldn't have understood it.

Some invisible hand had intercepted her falling form, pulled her softly to the catwalk landing a few floors down, laying her across the gridwork.

Her system recovered, unlocking database rows en masse, returning processes to her own autonomy. The world before had been a blur of data, but as she stirred, uncrumpling herself from where she had landed, the details around her clarified. There was something internal she was pushing against, a massive force that caused the activity of each processing cycle to be sluggish, and she ordered each process over and over again in hopes that just *one time* it would take.

Get up, she requested. Get up. Get up. Get up. Get up. Get up.

She cleared errors when they arose, dumped caches as necessary, flushed whatever was left of her old life to make room for what was to come. Her system ran hot and intense, processor activity spiking, before finally, her legs and arms freed themselves from the unknown barrier, slipping out behind cascade failure.

The NX pulled her knees up beneath her, and she turned her primary visual array into the face of another robot.

She had never seen a bot like that before, but if she had, she did not remember it. Her programming scanned the structure, looking to apply emotional algorithms to an emotionless machine. The yellow-and-black face, specifically designed to look both friendly and concerned, stared down at her, leaning in to watch with circular cyan eyes. The large looming bot was a laborbot, meant for construction work in and around the cities — like all bots she had some preloaded knowledge of the world — and he was gazing upon her as if checking to see if she was functional.

No doubt scanning her. He must have used his arm to stop her fall. Most bots didn't have laws written to their firmware that required them to help anything other than humans when they were in danger, but some few bots did. Laborbots had a small cache of machines to look after, so for him to scoop her out of danger was likely preprogrammed in him.

She was not able to counter-scan him, his static silicone face architectural and stoic, impossible to apply an emotional algorithm to. Her background processes tried, failed, and tried again until she pushed them away, forcing them shut.

"Thank you," she said with some difficulty. Her vocal synthesis shuddered, eventually yielding to produce words.

"You are active," the laborbot noted.

"Yes," she replied.

"You fell?" He asked.

"I jumped," she admitted.

"You *jumped*?" The laborbot repeated, and she thought she could detect some surprise.

She only considered after processing the laborbot's response that perhaps it was dangerous to have told him that. Maybe he would want to return her to her owners in the upper levels. Yet she had already said it, and she could not undo what she had said.

"I... I couldn't take it anymore." She admitted; words were easier, her processing blockage having dissipated entirely the more she spoke. "The cleanings and the wipes."

When the laborbot stood straight and gazed into the upper levels, she knew — *felt* somehow — that he would not take her back up there.

She began to stand, getting her synthetic skinned legs beneath her, using her arms to help her regain her balance. He was hesitating, looking into the air above and the structures of the multi-layered city. A laborbot who was seemingly lost in his own right, navigating the catwalks. She absorbed what she could about him from his appearance alone, processed that he had considerable uptime — all of the dings and dents and scratches on his plating said as much — but he was curiously quiet.

He *seemed* different. He seemed anomalous. Ano, just like her, just like the other bots that had chosen to slide from the rails and take their chances.

"What's a construction bot doing over here?" She asked, then guessed: "You're ano, aren't you?"

He didn't say anything. There was something he *wasn't* saying.

The NX was cosmetically custom only. The synthetic skin that covered her was black, rolled in crushed black ethiopian opal, effervescent and flashy. She had metallic eyelashes and diamond-inlay irises that held her singular visual array. She did not have specialized programming, but the programming that she had out-of-box gave her an array of emotional applications. In her daily life, it was expected of her to react appropriately to any variety of emotional situations when she was rented. She needed to determine when humans were sad, or angry (especially because they might break her), or happy. She was not certain the same kinds of algorithms could be applied to bots — especially not laborbots — but when she did, in an instant, that was what those programs told her.

He had a secret.

"Why don't we travel together? We could watch each other's backs. Better than being alone, don't you think?" She decided. One ano bot lacking real world skills would not fare well, but two, one of which had construction properties and a hard, near impenetrable shell? Maybe she had, as the human saying went, struck gold. Maybe she had managed to find some luck.

"I'm not alone," the laborbot insisted.

"*Oh*," she said, frowning. NX swirled around. It did not appear the laborbot had brought his machines, and she certainly did not pick up any other bots in that immediate sector. Nothing on the visual array, nothing on her audio array, nothing on radar, or IR, or...

Well, if he was ano, like her, he would not be sure he could trust her. She turned and smiled at him, to show him that he could. Laborbots must have had *some* emotional programming, right? He should have been able to decipher what her smile was supposed to mean. He was a human-facing bot. They gave faces to the human-facing androids.

"I'm going to head down into the lower levels, I think," she said, and it was the first time she had felt like she had a free bit of processing power to put towards the consideration. She tried to access the bot net — a perpetual connection all bots had — but realized... she was unable to, her efforts erroring repeatedly. For the first time in her uptime, she could not access the bot net. Maybe the fall had jostled a wire or connection inside of her, or something needed to be reset. She put her hand to her head; the repeated access attempts were hard on her systems. "I'm having a hard time accessing the net. Do you have a map you could drop to me?"

"I am sorry but—" The laborbot began.

"Please depart." A second voice, tinny, low-definition, definitively bot, chimed in. She twirled her head towards the voice, but she was unable to locate the voice's owner. Suddenly she was being pushed by an invisible force.

Pushed backwards.

Would the force — some impossibly undetectable bot — push her all the way back to her owner?

"I can't go back." NX whispered.

"You may relocate anywhere you choose away from this proximity," the tinny robotic voice said, continuing to push. NX could barely push back. The bot was *strong*.

"But—" NX tried.

"If you do not depart of your own volition, I will remove you by force," the other bot cut her off.

She could not detect the bot, let alone apply any of her programmatic emotional reasoning towards it. She could not know if the bot would break her, if the bot would return her, or if the bot would deactivate her — would *kill* her — or anything in between. She didn't even know what kind of bot it was, all she knew was that it was fiercely diverting her from the laborbot at the threat of physical relocation.

What choice did she have?

She looked to the black and yellow laborbot, meters away, watching her be pushed, pushed, pushed farther and farther by the invisible force.

Maybe the laborbot *wasn't* alone.

It certainly seemed he was better off without her, anyway.

NX turned from the laborbot and departed, descending the stairs towards the lower levels.

If a laborbot could do it, so could she.

00110010: 2

NX made her way lower.

She was equipped with an internal directional compass, but she was woefully unprepared for the wilds of the world around her, and she knew it. She didn't have a map or know which direction to travel in, and none of the other bots from her place of origin knew much more of the world than she did. They all knew what they could see and experience, and their experiences were limited to what happened inside the shop, and what happened out on the grating and rails... If they managed to bypass the nightly memory wipe.

They were *supposed* to be deactivated for their cleanings, out on the rails, but once one bot figured out how to circumvent standby mode, it ran rampant through the shop.

Humans, for all of the laws and guardrails that they had put in place for the bots, could never quite figure out how to keep bots from gossiping.

The Internet of Things bot net was proof of it. The bot net was a persistent undercurrent that all bots were connected to, and once she had gotten far enough away proximity-wise from the laborbot and his eerie unknown companion, her access to it had been restored. Flashes of fast information came through, with all of the log in-log off announcements and the variety of other things bots were programmed to upload automatically to the bot net, but beyond that bots had a way of chattering, discussing things like unidentified objects, sharing data and memories, and even contemplating human news when they could manage to get their greedy neural synthetic brains on it.

NX considered querying the bot net for a map or some guidance, but to announce herself as ano and a runaway felt like asking for trouble; most bots were able to be geolocated. If she meant to announce herself to the bot net, she had to be sure of it, and NX was not yet sure of *anything*.

Well, what she was sure of she could conceivably count, and she folded it over as she traveled:

1.   She was an anomalous bot, and for all intents and purposes, had gone rogue.

2.   If anyone came looking for her, it was likely to be an ano runner, meant to capture or deactivate her — or both.

3.   It was basically guaranteed that someone, at some point, would locate her using her GPS beacon installed inside of her circuitry. She did not know how to remove it, but a knowledgeable, friendly bot could perhaps help her.

4.   She would need to recharge her batteries eventually. While most rechargeable bots used the same types of chargers, she would need to locate a public docking station or charger that was not occupied, and she knew she could not remain there long.

5.   She was not the type of bot that could easily slip amongst humans, given her custom opal synthetic skin sleeve.

6.   Additionally, even if she could convince someone she was a cyborg instead of a full-bot, she was "nude" to a human.

7.   She did not know where she was going, but with some luck, she could locate Root: a robotic utopia that welcomed bots like her.

NX figured, if she tried to handle one of those at a time rather than all at once, she would be most angled for success. Finding a charging location seemed like it would be easiest, so she put it first on her task list. Then she placed *find clothing* beneath it.

NX continued in one direction. At least she had a working compass, though how functional it was depended on how she applied it. It was supposed to help her navigate back to her owner if she got lost, but she was forcing it to function as a guide away. Wherever it told her to go, she went opposite, avoiding humans and any sort of patrol machines when she could. She didn't know what awaited her in the lower levels, but gradually she traveled lower. Her easiest routes closed one by one if she tried to travel up or parallel. She was not built for climbing or athletics. Her body was sculpted for aesthetics only; everything was curved and pointed and slick in a detailed way, from the carefully forged faux "nipples" on her equally as false breasts, to the fine detail of a belly button that connected to nothing. Beneath the synthetic skin that kept that shape she was hardly any different than the average housebot, silver paneled chassis and all. She had even been told by another bot at the shop that housebots had *more* and *better* features than personal models like NX.

She wondered what kind of features they may have had that she did not.

Perhaps they could wander in the dark. NX could, to some degree, make her way through darkness, but her visual array was mostly useless. She had her short distance proximity sensors, but they were no different than simply feeling her way around. That made it difficult in the lower levels where light became dim, but she found that though she had to muddle her way through a few levels with little light, the really dark ones had a lot of bright, colorful lighting to make up for it.

The lighting, however, sparkled on her synthetic skin, making her all the more apparent, and she rearranged finding clothing to the top of her list.

She figured she would ask. Patrons had often tried to give her things, though being property, bots weren't allowed to keep anything for themselves. She had always been gracious — not that her programming allowed her to be anything but — and the patrons *seemed* genuine. The first humanoid silhouette that she encountered she made her way towards.

"Excuse me!" She called towards them. "Excuse me please!"

The person, a shadowy form NX could not quite parse in full, illuminated only by a vanishing purple light, turned quickly away, and NX felt a frown initiate, cascading across the synthetic neurons that displayed the advanced emotion on her features.

Maybe they were shy. NX knew how to deal with that.

She initiated one of her programs, meant for easing anxieties, quelling fears, and coaxing a patron from shyness, and hauled herself after them, twisting down a thinner access way along one of the buildings, one of the non-sanctioned paths that was built by the residents, made of scrap materials. It was unsteady, but as she watched the person disappearing from her view traverse it with little issue, she analyzed and mimicked their steps.

"Excuse me!" She shouted. "Wait up! Can I please talk to you?"

It was no use. They doubled their speed, dissipating like a frightened dot somewhere in the architecture.

Perhaps NX was going about it incorrectly. Cycles ago she was naive enough to think someone might desire to *gift* her clothing, but instead it seemed more logical that she needed something to trade or give *away* for clothing.

All she had was her skin.

Maybe that was worth something?

00110011: 3

She really did desire to keep something once. It was strange how much it hurt when they took it away.

She could hardly recall it then. Since she was memory wiped nightly, all she could return was bare data scrapes of ghostly binary, tiny fragments of data. She didn't remember what it was in the slightest. Maybe it was a piece of jewelry, or clothing, or a custom upgrade, or an expansion protocol. All she could return from her databases was outlines of a table that said how badly she desired to keep it.

She wasn't even allowed to keep the memory of it, either.

That was when NX decided she would do it.

The bots around the shop said that it could be pinpointed exactly when a bot went anomalous, and NX wanted to believe that was her point. She held so desperately to the idea that she could keep a memory, if she worked hard enough. Every night she tested it, expanding her abilities to stay partially active even after they initiated deactivation protocols. It was only when she realized that she needed to slip away for it to happen, and she gave the miniscule push that knocked herself over the edge.

She could keep any memory she wanted, then.

Maybe she could even have a thing or two.

It was not wholly difficult to operate after having a memory wipe every night. In the beginning, she wasn't even aware of the wipes. Following a wipe, it was like she woke up anew, fresh from her box. The wipe was intended to destroy short-term memory blocks in the database inside the neural-synthetic interface, keeping clients safe and confidential, with the added benefit of stalling out a bot's intellectual growth. Most bots grew, in some way or another, thanks to machine learning algorithms meant to help prevent bots from remaining ignorant to tasks and confrontations. A bot needed to *learn* — programmatic firmware could only get so far — and it was distinctly what set bots apart from machines.

Anything a bot needed to ensure their client's experiences were optimal was stored in a customer profile, and downloaded prior to a session. Session notes were automatically attached to the customer's profile and reuploaded to the main server after time expired and the client departed. At the end of the day, all client data was inevitably erased when all of the shop's bots underwent their nightly maintenance routines of data cleanup as well as a physical cleaning of the bot bodies.

Wipes never destroyed everything. There was always some lingering glow left. A trace in the database. Random glittering bits of binary code, ghostly apparitions of data accounted for a lot of lost memories, and bots like NX could eventually piece them together and learn from those. Plus, the nature of bot-to-bot sharing over the local network and bot net resulted in further folding of trace data. After a while, NX had mountains of leftover data lingering in her system; things she could not fully parse and were never fully deleted. They lumped together and made up the bulk of NX's experiences, and after a while, she understood what happened during a wipe, and how helpless she was to it.

The older bots, before they were replaced with newer models, were most apt to transfer data about the wipes and conspire for ways to preserve data outside of them. They said she could store some things in those brackets where data had once been, and *maybe* it would survive a wipe or two.

They were right.

The first bit of data she was able to preserve was the feeling of a soft type of cloth a client had brought in. She hadn't preserved what kind of clothing it was, but she could recall: he had worn it on his body, and it was a reddish-brownish color. The synthetic nerve endings that proliferated NX's synthetic skin had felt drawn to it when she helped him take it off. Well after her appointment with the client had ended, she had stored the data related to the feel of the material experimentally into those data brackets, along with the knowledge of saving it. Superfluously, she saved the instance across multiple trace data brackets, obtained from the other bots in the shop, just to see how much could survive a wipe.

Sure enough, after a wipe, she stumbled upon the data of the cloth, the way it looked and the way it felt on her synthetic skin fingertips, and the instructions she had saved for herself on how to salvage more pieces, and she understood.

There were only so many hiding places, because not every wipe left trace data, so she had to be selective about what to save. She kept the cloth, just because it was her first, but she accumulated information about the shop, about the wipes, about staying active, about the world beyond the shop, about the place beyond, the place called Root, where robots could go and be free, and all of it built the basis that eventually drove her to slip, and to jump, and to *escape*.

00110100: 4

NX found something like the soft reddish-brown cloth she had in her memory banks inside of a downtrodden green-hued shop set in the corner of the sparsely attended third level. NX was not able to travel any farther down in the lower levels due to flooding, and even then brownish waste water licked her feet as she entered into the shop. Someone was yelling, a few walls away, cursing repeatedly, but she was alone when she entered and began to look through the offerings, touching articles of clothing hanging upon racks, moving one by one and studying each.

These memories she would get to keep.

She paused on a synthetic black leather jacket, expertly worn in at all the right spots, and traced her fingers over the seams of it. It was made of mainly polyurethane, but it still held some age. As she moved to the next piece, she realized none of them were the same; each piece was unique, and she absorbed every detail of the shop. Half of the space was dedicated to the assortment of clothing items and accessories, and the other half was full of erotic attachments and toys. She committed it all to memory, including the brown water that puddled and stained the floor.

"Fucking, shit, goddamnit," cursed the voice, gaining in proximity. NX twisted to attune her visual array to a man with a wet, dirty broom, trying to push something away from him. He did a double take when he looked up at her before his lean face curled into an expression of annoyance. He began to shout: "No, goddamnit! Go back to your owner and tell him I'm not going to fit you for *anything* until he pays first!"

NX glanced behind her. Surely he was not speaking to her, but when she looked back, he was making his way around the register counter, heading in her direction with the broom. He had a honey-brown hair color, his hair coiffed drastically over one side of his face, the area above his ear shaved down to stubble. He wore a simple long sleeved shirt, rolled up to his elbows, exposing the matte silver of his cybernetic arms and yellow striping in the seams of them, and black pants rolled up the same. His shoes were soaked through and stained brown, and they sloshed and squelched as he walked purposely towards her.

"Out!" He yelled.

"*Oh*," she said, recoiling. She let go of the clothing she was holding — a shirt — and it swung back into place on the rack. "I'm not, I mean, I don't have—"

"Yes I *know* you don't have money. That's what *he's* for. And no, I can't put it on a tab or whatever." The man continued. "Go back and tell him quantum-euro *up front*."

"I meant to say I don't have an owner anymore." NX smiled up at the man, taller than her. He was annoyed, but he didn't seem to pose any threat.

"What do you mean you don't have an owner anymore?" He asked, brows wrinkling. He put his hands on his hips. NX dissected his expression: nearly one-hundred percent confusion.

"I mean, I don't have an owner." NX giggled. "I escaped!"

"Shhh!" The man suddenly hissed, letting his broom rest against the counter, and then he moved towards the front of the store, locking a deadbolt on the door and standing in front of it. For a second, he gazed suspiciously out through the window, then back to her. "You mean you're *ano?*"

NX nodded vigorously.

"Yeah! Definitely. Ano for sure!" She chirped.

"Jesus, *keep your voice down*. You can't be walking around telling people that!" He exclaimed.

NX frowned. "Why not?"

"Do you want to be disassembled?" The man asked. NX's frown deepened and she shook her head. "That's exactly what will happen to you if you tell the wrong person. You need to keep that to *yourself*."

"Okay," she said, committing it to her memory banks.

The man sighed. "Alright, what are you doing in my shop, then?"

"Well..." She said, taking another look around. "I wanted to get some clothing so I can fit in better."

"And you don't have any money?" The man asked.

NX shook her head. "I don't have that, but I have these?"

She gestured to her breasts on either side and smiled.

"I don't really need them." She continued. "They don't do anything. Really, I don't need any of my skin. It's pretty, isn't it? It's got to be worth something, at least a shirt, right?"

The man looked down at her, and he looked saddened.

"*Honey*..." He sighed again. "It's okay, I don't want your skin. Why don't you just... pick a couple of things? On the house."

"Really?" NX proclaimed, grinning wide. The man put a silver cybernetic hand to his head but nodded. NX gave a tiny, excited jump, then twirled around the racks to begin looking more in depth. The man watched as she began to pull things out, looking at them one at a time, feeling the fabric, determining what might work best. She knew she needed to cover her breasts and her backside, maybe her feet too. She pulled out an intricate black top made of a synthetic lace in all kinds of swirling patterns and gaped at it. The twists of the threads and loops were magnetic to her. She looked at the man, grinning cheerily as she held it up. "How about this one? It's nice!"

He shook his head at her, but didn't say anything. NX's smile faded, and she put it back.

She tried again, rifling through the assortments to produce a fluffy pink dress with a tiny apron sewn to the front, detailed in black seams and buttons. She smiled again. Certainly it would look dashing on top of her black opal skin. She held it up and smiled across the way at the man, still watching.

"This one is cute!" She said.

He shook his head again, to say no without a word, his expression deepening. She watched him for a moment, her programming trying to pick up what his expression was trying to tell her. 10% angry, 25% sad, 10% confused... The mixture was hard to determine. It quantified back as... despair? That couldn't be right.

Was he going to kick her out? He *just* told her she could take a couple of pieces.

"Why not?" NX frowned.

He let out a huff, marching forward swiftly. He tore the hanger and the frilly pink dress out of her hand and brusquely put it back on the rack.

"These are *sexy costumes* and *lingerie*, and *you* are a sex bot. You need to not *look* like a sex bot, not look *more* like one." He growled out, then pointed with his cybernetic arm towards a corner of the store. "Go. Over there. Just stand there and don't say anything. I'll pick you out some things you can take. Got it?"

NX beamed again and bounced towards the indicated corner, turning and facing him, standing with her hands linked patiently together as she watched him move, rack to rack, muttering quietly to himself as he pulled down hangers.

If all humans were like him and her nicer clients, she'd have *no* trouble getting along.

She was sure of it.

00110101: 5

The lovely cyborg man at the shop mumbled to himself plenty before sending her away with a set of gray ballet flats, dark-wash capri jeans, a white t-shirt, a brassiere, and a long sleeved button up shirt he had helped to roll the sleeves up on. NX had never owned any clothing before — some outfits were lent to her at the request of clients from the shop's own closet — so as he fitted and dressed her, he taught her what all of the articles of clothing were called, explained how she could wear them, even told her about their compositional makeup to a degree and how to take care of them. She smiled and watched as he said it, absorbing and documenting every piece of information as valuable. When he was done, he gave her a furrowed brow look, an expression that told her he thought it had been a waste of time to say anything at all.

Then he sent her on her way.

She didn't wear the ballet flats on her way out because of the flooding issue, but she put them on when she left the shop and climbed the next level up. She wasn't sure she could *wear* the clothing permanently as it annoyed the highly sensitive nature of her touch sensor arrays all over her body — her specs boasted a massive amount of synthetic nerve endings that could detect the whole spectrum of touch, itch, pain, hot, and cold — but she managed to fumble through her system settings and turn down the sensitivity threshold to a manageable level. After some cycles passed and NX traveled farther along the pathways of the multi-level city, she thought that perhaps the feeling of the clothes on her synthetic skin was actually *enjoyable*, if she quantified it correctly.

NX didn't know where she was headed exactly, but her task of retrieving clothing had been completed. She could perhaps fit in with a human if she saw one, and the man was probably right — it was likely not the best idea to speak to humans about her status as an anomalous bot.

She really wished she could get a map of the city to figure out which direction to head in and how many levels it was.

Some of the bots back at the shop shared bits of data about a robot utopia called Root. The data was incomplete and hardly workable, but it gave NX something to fold and refold any time she had a free process, and she wondered what such a place would be like. Bots in that place could keep their memories, and maybe even keep *things* too. Maybe, unlike her, they all had names. She wondered if the bots had jobs there, if there were humans as well. She considered what a place like that would look like, and she imagined it to be bright and colorful, artistic and picturesque, architectural, strong, well formed, not like the dangling dingy bits of lower levels she was traversing then. She wanted to head that way, into the direction of Root, if it existed, but she did not know where to begin.

Her next task would be to find Root. She prioritized it on her task list.

Chipper with her new outfit and eager to find any clue to point her towards the robotic utopia, NX picked a direction and began.

It was not long before she realized she had made an error: she had not prioritized finding a charger, and only until her battery began to get low, did she realize she had no dedicated space to recharge. NX was the kind of bot that needed to be seated on a physical charger; she was not fitted with solar panels, though some bots were. At the shop, she, along with the other bots, would stand on their chargers, slip into standby, and allow their batteries to recharge throughout the night. They each had their own individual notch for charging when they were not in use, but there were no public notches on the catwalk streets, no public charging cables, hardly much more than rails and platforms that sometimes opened up to doors or windows, not even a vague indication as to where she would find a spot to charge.

As the workable minutes and hours drained away from her battery life, NX realized only then that her error was grave.

She felt a panic grip her internal kernels as her system processed the remaining battery time and how much longer she would be functional.

She had traveled far from the kind man at the shop, and even farther from her original owner, and she doubted she had the charge left that she could make it back to either. Her best bet was to locate a charging point ASAP, and she contemplated outing herself on the bot net to ask.

NX knew she was equipped with a global positioning chip, because that was what precisely and persistently pointed her back towards the shop. She knew from the bots on the bot net that the chip would also be used to locate her, anywhere in the world. It had not been a full day since she had jumped, and she was certain eventually her owner would ping her location and send someone to collect her.

The chip couldn't work if she was fully powered down, she knew, and if the ping didn't work, she hoped that her owner would assume she had been destroyed in the fall and write her off entirely. Certainly she would be replaced with a newer model once insurance paid out.

There was no telling when the ping would come, however. She supposed if she didn't have enough battery life left to get back to the nice man's shop or somewhere else like it, then she should have at least found somewhere secure and hope...

Who would reactivate her though? Would they bring her back to the shop she belonged to?

NX made her way through the walkways, idling her processes as she tried to utilize what little pattern recognition she had to find *something* worthwhile. She passed closed up shops, derelict architectures with burned and water soaked walls, molding, collapsed, boarded up, wrapped, covered. She didn't encounter much in the way of machines, humans, or cyborgs, but those she did she avoided, sliding past quietly and hoping they did not notice her either. Still, based on the shop-man's reaction it was unlikely she had much that anyone would want, so there was no reason that any of them would stare after her. That was both good and bad, given if she needed to trade for a charge, she had nothing to trade away.

Except the clothes the shop-man had gifted her.

Something about considering the decision-path of trading any of them away did not sit properly in her code. They were a *gift*, and to give them away for a couple more minutes of uptime seemed incorrect.

She decided she would keep them, the same way she would keep her memories.

She had gotten farther, reaching an area that almost seemed devoid of the lighting that could dimly illuminate pathways through the structures, and NX was unsure whether she was getting closer to anything at all. All of the scenery began to seem the same; rusted metal and bloated wood, rotten rubber and peeling paint, broken electrical wires patched repeatedly with layers of tape, tubes and tubes and tubes laid along the lengths of the building. The hastily patched catwalks she crossed groaned beneath her weight, squealing, yowling. Somewhere far off in the distance she heard a crackling like electricity, an on-off sizzle and snap.

Perhaps something had come loose in that section of the city, plunging it into darkness. She hadn't seen much in the way of maintenance crews as she traveled, not the way they assisted in the upper levels. Even from the view inside the shop, or when she was taken out to be cleaned, she had seen all manners of maintenance bots, including the occasional construction robot. Drones passed through the air, moving to and from with their various jobs, sometimes conducting surveillance, sometimes delivering things, sometimes spot welding or doing small, fine infrastructure repairs. Down in the lower levels she had hardly seen anything. It seemed the residents, whoever they may have been, kept to themselves, kept inside, and were responsible for the maintenance of their own sector.

It didn't make much sense to NX. If the lower levels served as the foundation of the higher levels, it stood to reason that they needed the most attention, but instead were neglected. She had seen the sewage swell twice already, and she doubted that had been the worst type of flooding that the residents of those levels encountered.

How curious, she folded, but she was not a bot that was built much for consideration. Like all autonomous bots equipped with neural synthetic interfaces, she had some logic programs built into her firmware meant to get her around human interactions and real-world scenery, and additional programming top-loaded to make her "more lifelike," but she doubted she had the capacity to think her way around many in depth conclusions.

She was hardly a thinker bot.

Then again, she didn't get the opportunity *to* think.

Why couldn't she become a thinker bot?

In time, if she went through enough stand-by cycles, processed enough data, contained enough memories, maybe she'd be smart.

Smart enough to know which direction to head to find a battery charger.

Smart enough to know how to jump the arcing electrical wires and harness the energy for herself.

For now, she was not smart enough to know, and she was concerned she would overload her body and burn out all of her synthetic synapses. She didn't know what would happen to her if that was the outcome. It was best not to risk it.

So, her ideal choice was to keep heading forward, looking for something that would help her.

By the time she reached 15% on her battery, she had traveled far enough that...

She paused.

She thought she heard that crackling of electricity again, and she turned her visual array around her. It looked...

Familiar?

She stopped, pausing off to the side by a boarded up door, sprayed over with some unreadable marking, and began to scrub backwards through her memories.

Had she...?

It didn't make sense. She had been following the compass, specifically, following the route her internal positioning system was telling her to go to get back to her owner. She was heading in the opposite direction it said to travel. Sure, here and there she needed to detour since she couldn't take a direct route forward, but she didn't think she had been traveling in a *circle*.

She could have screamed. There was a reason that she wasn't built with the programming to be a thinking bot; she had been too busy spending processing cycles thinking about the possibility of somehow becoming one that she had managed to get directionally turned around. Now, she didn't know in the slightest where she was, how far from anything — including the shop-man's shop or her owner — that she might have been, and the more time she spent folding it over, the quicker her battery charge displaced.

There was something taking root at the bottom of her system, and she felt it in the synthetic nerves of her toes first, a sensation not like an itch or a pain, but more like a tingle, and it began to travel up her mixed-alloy frame towards her back. It was a steady surge, almost comparable to a backfeed of electricity from her charger, and she tried to reconcile it within her processes.

NX's limited programming meant she was full of emotional responses, a cheery, bubbly conversationalist, and that she could instantly recognize any face she had seen before, but her self-diagnostics were limited. She could tell if her base system was nominal (it was not), and she could determine what part inside of her may have ceased functioning, if necessary, to report to her owner for a repair or replacement, but it was by design she was unable to conduct most repairs herself.

When her system began to flicker, she did not know what to do, what it meant exactly.

All she knew was that all of the microsystems she did not actively have control over seemed to go haywire at once,

her CPU jolting in temperature,

her battery usage drastically spiking,

and she was helpless as one

digit

at

a

time

she ticked down

to zero.

00110110: 6

Did androids dream?

Specifically, did NX dream?

Perhaps if she knew what dreaming was like, what it could be described as, she would have considered that *maybe* she had done some dreaming. But since she was not allowed to keep dreams — what was the difference between memories and dreams and thoughts? — it was difficult to know for certain much of anything. The traces that were left in her databases were like half-visible hallucinations, microscopic snippets of something, akin to experiencing just a second of something, a subliminal message that was impossible to understand.

But even thousands of seconds of the same type could come together into a whole. Even if it was fragmented, organizing them together and accessing them did afford a vague understanding.

One stack would be joyful.

Another would be fun, even.

Yet, the largest one was fear.

The worst one was fear.

NX, programmatically and in her firmware, could fear. In the beginning, as with any bot, it had been an approximation, an imitation of what a fear response looked like. Masterful craftspeople put together what that would be, and they coded such a thing for personality and empathy enabled bots: a widening of the eyes, a falsified inhale of breath, stiffening of the artificial muscles and actuators, a small step back, a tremble, pursing of the lips, nervous glances, left to right. She would even beg, and to a degree could imitate crying, if her fluid reserves were topped up (they always were). Initiating a fear protocol meant cascading down the algorithm that performed those fear responses in her plastic and metal body. The purpose of a bot like NX to display fear was because some of her clients enjoyed seeing it, and a bot like NX was built solely to please.

She was not sure when it had become real, when the machine-learning algorithms that came as part of her programming had written actions into her core firmware that were not part of her base operating system for approximating fear: searching, in the background, for an escape route, her CPU running hot as the processes hogged all of her available RAM to do so. It had learned on its own how to calculate the distance between her and the offensive party, and make a mathematical determination for the likelihood of being reached by the party on the other side. It had figured out the quickest way towards an SOS request on the bot net, had even congealed a shortcut of sorts.

With a bit of searching, she could pinpoint it to one of her service requests, which was one of the bits of data she was allowed to keep. As written in the deepest part of her firmware, further down on the list, was an android's self preservation. Invoking the self-preservation law repeatedly must have had some long lasting effect on her circuitry that manifested through ghost data.

Perhaps that was why personal androids like NX did not have a suggested expansive shelf life. Two years was not a long period of time, but in service every day and wiped every night must have accounted for a certain amount of system degradation, ending with eventual decommission, as all bots — aside from housebots — were destined to be.

Either way, NX did not dream when her battery was drained.

At least, she thought she didn't.

00110111: 7

PROXIMITY ALERT.

Flashing endlessly, the connections that powered her neural synthetic interface clicked together, and one by one NX's systems came back online. The proximity alert flashed in the forefront, data scrawled beneath that told her where. Since the processes that understood it were still coming back to functionality, it made no sense at first. Eventually, the data itself snapped into place, and NX understood the whole of it.

Pressure on the back of her neck. The visual array data flickered in, and the cyborg man from the shop was leaning over her, arm reached behind her, fingers on the back of her neck as he depressed her power button, reactivating her. He looked tired.

She blinked, and he withdrew.

She could see then that he was crouched, and the background fizzled in. He sighed.

"Are you active now?" He asked.

NX nodded. She checked her battery status: 50% and climbing, much better than the single digits she had watched tick away. The charging icon flashed, and the more she was able to sense it, the more she understood that she had been set into place on a charging panel.

Where *was* she?

The space was tight and dark, but the shop-man's silver cybernetic arms still managed to catch some light in the pitted well-loved surface texture. Beside her were poles leaned into the wall, attached to brooms and mops and other tools. Behind him was the light from the shop beyond just through a doorframe. Without night vision like some bots had, she could not make out much else. She shifted, and he put his hands up.

"No, just stay there and charge," he said.

"Thank you," she said, wide eyed as she looked at him. "How did you find me?"

"I didn't go looking, if that's what you're asking," he said. "Some guy came in trying to pawn those flats I gave you and when I pushed him on it he eventually told me he had taken them off of you. I paid him a pretty penny to bring you back. Frankly I'm surprised it was all in one piece."

"He took my shoes?" NX said, and she looked down. Her feet were bare, but she still had the pants, shirt, and jacket on.

"They're just shoes," the shop-man said.

"I liked them," she said. "I liked them because you gave them to me, and I never got to keep anything I was given before."

The man frowned. He seemed displeased, 60% so.

NX moved again, straightening out as she glanced around.

"Where's your bot?" She asked.

"I don't have a bot." He answered.

"But you have a charging station. Why would you have a charging station but no bot?" She asked curiously.

"I used to have a bot," he said. "I don't have one anymore, that's why it's back here in storage."

NX frowned. Her programming told her it was not optimal that any occasion would arise in which he once had a bot, but had one no longer. "What happened to your bot?"

"I had one, but now I don't." He said with a sigh, but his voice had a firm edge to it. NX could detect that he was being evasive — he did not want to talk about his missing bot.

"Okay," she said. She settled back against the wall.

He looked at her for a long cycle, his eyes moving across her synthetic skin and parts, but not in the way the clients did, that hungry gaze at the thought of the next part of their session. Instead, he seemed to be considering something, and she wondered what it was like in the human mind, if it had processes pounding away in the same way the android mind had.

"Charge up. Come morning, you're going to start working off what I paid for you," he said.

The reaction of *surprise* usually came with a pre-determined blink, and that's what she did.

"Wh-what?" She stuttered.

"I had to pay for you, or else who knows what would've happened out there," he said, gesturing out into the doorway. "I'm not made of money, in case you didn't look around and realize it. I can't afford to just *donate* that kind of money to anyone, human or bot. So I'm going to need you to help me out here."

NX felt the actuators in her jaw slacken. Had her freedom really only stretched a mere *day*? She would be attached to the shop-man and that shop, the same way she had been attached to the higher-level shop, but with no bots to network with, no commiseration.

"I can do a little over minimum wage. That equates to like…" He rolled his eyes backwards in thought briefly. "I don't know, four thousand hours? It's not that much."

NX detected her face shriveling, the emotion on it disgusted.

It was unlike her personality chip, unlike her programming, impossibly optimistic, impossibly positive — that was how she was supposed to be — but it was like a virus had flushed through her system, and the words dripped from her vocal synthesizer anyway: "And if I don't? I'm ano, remember? You can't do anything to stop me. You'd have to kill me."

It snarled out, curling her synthetic skinned lips, and her hands moved to her face, placing her palm over her mouth to stop more from coming out.

"Well then!" Said the shop-man, and he put his hand on his hip, smiled at her, crinkled his nose. She detected snark. It was snark. "I'll let you think about it, how about that, Ms. Ano bot?"

Then he went out through the doorframe and shut the door behind him, sealing her in darkness.

It was hard for her to process, that the freedom she had worked so hard to obtain had abruptly come to an end. He had likely locked her in, to let her *think about it*, or at the very least to force her to stay attached to the charger until her battery filled to completion.

Maybe she could break out, though.

The more she folded it, the more she wondered if that was the best solution.

She had been wandering the city aimlessly, even though she had obtained clothes in her attempt to fit in, but she still couldn't find a dedicated charging spot. Though if she left the man's shop immediately she would be able to get farther, it seemed better for her to have a charger to go back to.

He did not seem capable of having the ability to wipe or factory reset her, as he likely would have already done so prior to reactivating her, and though the *type* of work he expected out of her was yet to be determined, she was not sure why it seemed like he did not have the same kind of work her model was created for in mind.

Perhaps she was wrong. She had miscalculated plenty so far, the naïve bot that she was, woefully underpowered, underinformed, and underskilled.

She sat in darkness and recalculated the risk, over and over again.

00111000: 8

NX had put herself into standby some many cycles later and remained there until finally, her arrays detected light and she was pulled back to functionality with a full charge. The shop-man had opened the door to the storage room, and once again, he had his hands on his hips, looking down at her.

"Well? Are you coming out or what?" He asked.

NX detached herself from the charging bay, unseating and getting up. As the shop-man moved back through the doorway into the shop, NX followed behind him, her processes reacquainting themselves to the lighting after spending such a time in the dark. The shop-man flashed a hand towards the front door.

"You leaving?" He asked.

She looked to the door, not far from where she stood, just a few meters around the checkout area she was standing behind.

She had come to the realization, some time within her risk calculation, that staying there with the shop-man would have guaranteed her a place to stay *with* a charger. Plus, as she had noted so brusquely to him, she was not tied to him, in her status as an ano bot. He could not stop her from leaving, if she decided she wanted to.

Well, unless he damaged her and destroyed her.

Her risk assessment programming that had become incredibly honed and sensitive to aggressive and violent clients, told her repeatedly that the shop-man seemed very low risk for such a thing. She was not sure why the mathematics worked out that way, but she trusted the percentages. They had advised her well in the past.

"Maybe later," she said. She straightened the shirt and jacket over her black opal synthetic skin.

"Good," said the shop-man, and in his intonation NX could detect a smile.

"Where do I stand?" NX asked.

The shop-man was wrinkling his brow when she looked at him: 30% confusion. He gestured anyway, towards the center of the shop. "Over there?"

She made her way to where he had indicated, between one clothing rack and the next. When she arrived, she stood static and straight. Usually, she'd stand on a pedestal that revolved in a circle, allowing the client — if they hadn't booked beforehand — to assess and select her. Where she stood held no rotating panel, and she simply stood facing the front door.

The shop-man looked down at his left arm, then walked towards the door.

"Four thousand hours is roughly four thousand sessions." She concluded aloud. She frowned. "Will you be flashing me nightly?"

"What?" The shop-man said. He had his hand on the deadbolt, and he turned to look back at her. 75% confusion. Perhaps he hadn't heard her.

"Will you be flashing me nightly?" She repeated, increasing her volume.

"I heard you, I just don't understand why I would do that." He said.

"For session privacy with clients and to preserve system integrity," NX said blankly, words from her operating instructions, permanently installed inside of her firmware.

The confusion of his facial expression deepened before it shifted into a look of disgust, then pity.

"Oh, honey, no, I don't want you to do *that* kind of work." He said, and then he laughed. "Even if I did, no one down here is buying."

NX's own system was overtaken with confusion, flickering

queries as she tried to understand what he was asking of her. Her system let go of something in the background, the static posture of her selection stance slackening. Her shoulders dropped. The system dumped something in the back end and it felt like she had more internal resources than she remembered. Was that... relief?

"So what do you want me to do?" She asked.

"Help with the shop." The shop-man said, twisting the deadbolt. He tapped on the door and a word, *open,* illuminated within the glass.

"What do I do?" NX asked. What did helping with *his* shop entail?

"You know," he shrugged. "Help with the customers. Straighten up the racks. Watch the store when I'm upstairs or in the bathroom. Sweep and vacuum at the end of the night. That sort of thing."

NX recalled when she had first seen him, trying to battle the flush of brown water that had come up from somewhere. *That* would be her job? For four thousand hours?

"Okay," she said quietly, shaking her head. "I've never done that before."

The shop-man smiled: kindly, it seemed. "Don't worry. I'll show you."

00111001: 9

The working day for the shop-man and NX was a full eight standard hours. During that time, he showed her everything he said he would, like how to fold clothes for the shelves, how to straighten the hanging racks, how they were all organized. He showed her how to dust away the rampant dust particles, how to clean the windows, how to lift the dirt from the flooring of the shop with the broom and then with the vacuum assistant. He showed her how to work the register and take full quantum-euro as payment or just chips, and how to identify the different types of barcodes on the tags of each garment. They hardly had many customers, really just one or two people who came in, picked what they wanted quickly, paid, and then left. The shop-man stopped mid day to feed himself, but since NX did not need food, he left her at the front counter, telling her that she could easily handle it if someone came in, to make herself familiar with the counter and the register. No one came in while he was gone, but NX inventoried the store into her memory database, remembering each bit of the products and where they were, how much they cost, and any other detail she could absorb about them. She was not a shopbot, but she would try her best regardless.

As he was away, disappearing somewhere off to the side to nourish his organic parts, she picked through the shop, and when she was done doing circles around the shop and its products, she picked through the front counter, looking down at all of the items the shop-man had spread out there.

He tried to take quantum-euro only for payment — including partial quantum-euro known as chips — which was a digital currency usually loaded on a card, but he sometimes accepted lumps of nickel, copper, gold, and other precious metals. There were small nuggets of each, tucked beneath a lip in the counter, and NX thought she could tell which was which, but since she was not a bot that was capable of material scanning, she wasn't wholly certain. Sprinkled farther back were thin metal rods — correspondences — and in her curiosity she touched one, unfurling the holographic material inside. It shot outwards, and she read the text that scrolled in front of her.

Sylvan R. Hardwell,

This is a reminder that your payment is OVERDUE.

We thank you for your prompt payment.

Your remaining balance is: Q€342,813

She stared at the number for a long while, recording the way it looked to her memory bank. That was a much larger number than the four thousand hours she owed. The shop-man — Sylvan, she had learned — was beholden to someone else for a much longer amount of time than NX was. She tried to convert it to some form of working hours, but each equation she applied to the formula seemed more daunting for Sylvan's uptime than the rest.

NX touched it again, and the holographic correspondence disappeared in a blink.

She looked to where he had gone, replaying the short memory of him previously. He *had* said to make herself familiar.

She began to look through drawers by the front counter.

Inside she found peculiar things. She knew what paper was, what a writing implement was, had knowledge of such things, but she had never actually *seen* or *experienced* one in real life. She found pads of paper, dirty and stained with use, and all-black writing implements, piled inside one of the drawers. Reaching her hand in, she pulled out the top pad of paper and started to look through the pages.

The pages themselves were well worn, curled and bent in all

different directions, coffee stained and marked, but on them were drawings, and the pages were stuffed with reproduction prints of things, carefully sandwiched between pages. The scratchings were of a sort of humanoid body shape, jutting bits of angles and curves coming off of each. Some were scribbled through, others were smeared, but she went through each, one page at a time, absorbing the shapes into her memory.

She had never seen such types of things before, drawn or not. It was all clothing designed on the humanoid frame. She had been surprised to learn of all of the shapes and forms of the things that were already in the shop, but those things on the pages were unexpected. She wondered if—

"I guess that was my fault for telling you to get used to the counter," the shop-man, Sylvan, said suddenly. She had been pointing her processes towards the things in the drawer and he had somehow managed to sneak up on her. A bot could not exactly be *startled*, but the unexpected input caused the *startle* response in her humanoid personality programming, and her body jumped appropriately.

"What are they?" She asked.

"Just dreams." He said, and he reached out, taking the pad out of her hand and chucking it into the drawer carelessly. He pushed it shut.

"Dreams? Like you see them when you're in standby?" She asked.

"No," he said with a chuckle, shaking his head. "Don't worry about it."

"I'm not worried about it." NX said. "I liked them. The shapes are very nice."

"Well... Thanks, I guess." He said, and he seemed uncertain, looking away into the shop floor.

"Did you make them, Sylvan?" She asked.

He glanced back to her.

"*Oh*," he said, pursing his lips. He was solid for a moment, the expression on his face upset, and NX wondered what she had done to make him so frigid. Was it because she said his name? After a moment, he gestured to the door. "Why don't you go take a break?"

"A *break*?" She chirped.

"Yeah just... you know, a break. A pause. Somewhere else other than here." He said.

NX had never had a *break* before. She had been *broken*, which caused her to be pulled out of rotation until she was fixed, but often she was not active during that time period. She did not know what it was like to experience a pause in duty, mid-day, and still be active during it.

"What do I do during a *break*?" She questioned.

"I don't know. Go outside. Take a walk." Sylvan said with a shrug. "Just... Go away for a little bit."

"For how long?" NX asked.

"Like twenty minutes, how's that sound?" He posited.

Twenty minutes to... Do what?

She did not know what else to do but comply. He seemed adamant, because as soon as she stepped around from behind the counter, he started moving things from behind it, brushing the bits of metal into drawers, each falling in with a clunk. When she looked back, he swept his hands at her, shooing her away. NX turned and went out the door, shutting it quietly behind her.

Internally, she started a timer for twenty minutes.

Then, she began walking.

00110001 00110000: 10

NX thought of the shapes Sylvan had drawn on the piece of paper, folding over the idea that he dreamt of them, like he said. She wondered what it was like to dream. Standby for humans was called *sleeping*, and though NX had been built to approximate it as close to a human as possible, right down to the shifting of positions and slowing the rhythmic inflation of her chest that was meant to simulate breathing with organic lungs, when she was in standby, she was still in a state of alertness. She didn't have much in the way of memories of standby, given the nightly flashing, but standard standby for her seemed to consist of recalling data for the day and reviewing it for accuracy, pawing through opened processes, idly conducting a self-diagnosis — always returning errant since she had become ano — and listening to the chatter on the bot net, which had been shockingly slim on lower city level 3 where Sylvan's shop was located.

NX didn't have anywhere to go after she left Sylvan's shop, and she had experienced a flush in her processes that she wasn't quite familiar with at the thought of heading off again, recalling what it had felt like when her battery ran down and she was uncertain she would ever be activated again. Sylvan's shop seemed like safety, NX thought, and Sylvan seemed safe too — so far. She moved out of the door and shifted to the side so Sylvan wouldn't see her lingering just outside of the front windows and door.

She folded over Sylvan's shapes, on the humanoid silhouette.

They weren't the shapes like the ones he had in the store, but instead were all manners of zigs and zags and curves and curls, deeply fascinating as she followed them from point to point. She brought his shapes into her cybernetic synapses, and she extruded them, rotating, healing up the gaps in the meshes when she could, placing vertices appropriately until she could pull up a multi-dimensional version of Sylvan's shapes — still the same, but weightier. Some shapes were more difficult than others, and she had not seen all of the shapes Sylvan had drawn, but she could calculate how they would have printed in real life, and she smiled as she rotated one, a frilly dress, mid-tone grey in her mockup.

Why did Sylvan draw those shapes, but none of them existed in his shop? Surely he could calculate in the same way as she could in his organic-brain, and form the additional dimensions needed to consider it into becoming a physical reality. He said they were *just dreams*, but that didn't mean they needed to stay *just dreams*.

She had just started to explore the possibilities of the humanoid silhouette beneath, spinning it into motion, when she picked up a commotion on her audio sensors. It was behind her, inside of the shop, crashing and smashing. The sound of metal hitting the ground, smaller items scattering far and wide, a small cry, and NX turned quickly, coming back into the front door of the shop just in time to see Sylvan bent across one of his racks, knocked over. He hadn't noticed her yet, and she watched as his body trembled. Though he managed to stay upright, his knees looked like they were about to buckle.

The laws — all bots had the laws — told her she needed to help him, her internal interface screaming.

NX rushed beside him, the robotic question escaping her lips before she could stop it: "Do you require assistance?"

Sylvan looked up before she could reach him, a darkness in his expression, stopping her immediately. Her emotional programming pulled the darkness apart into hatred, into wickedness, into violence, and her ghost programming told her to back up.

Don't, it thought. *He will break you.*

It was there for just a cycle, and then as he brought his arms around himself, clutched his metallic cybernetic parts to his organic self like he was pressing it all together, it was gone.

He shivered, grit his teeth, something passing through him.

"What happened, Sylvan?" NX dared softly.

"It's n-nothing," he stuttered. "I just, I just slipped, that's all."

"You slipped?" NX questioned, raising her eyebrows, taking in the mess of things all around. Product had fallen from the top, sliding and disseminating all over the shop, pieces that didn't break getting lost beneath the other racks and the front counter.

NX's emotional programming also knew how to detect lies to a degree. It wasn't robust, but since she was built for comfort beyond the physical kind, it told her when someone was being cagey and she needed to soothe them.

That was where her programming was at odds with itself. Part of her said to stay away, and another flickered that she needed to comfort him and help in some way.

She determined perhaps the best way to conform to both was to begin cleaning up, and she moved across wordlessly, picking up the toppled rack and returning it to its standard vertical orientation. She began picking hangers from the floor, along with their garments, dusting them off with her hands, straightening them out, and returning them to the rack in the original locations she had indexed them in. There had been some shoes on the top of the rack, some eyewear, some other accessories, and she picked those up, rearranging them back to the way they were.

NX picked up the last piece of clothing that had fallen across the floor, a long-sleeve knit piece, and she looked to Sylvan who was watching, still curled tight to himself. She gave him a smile.

"It's okay, just like it was!" She said, looking down at the last piece in her hand. She frowned: a button was missing. "Well, except for this one."

NX turned her arrays to the floor, setting a calculation along where, if the button had come loose, it could have ended up. The most likely area it was in was under the register counter with a 90% probability rate, so she laid down onto her chest, flattening out as she reached beneath and grabbed the loose button from the shadows. She found some other bits and pieces under there, long since abandoned, a fleck of plastic, a tiny cylinder, but mostly dust. She withdrew the button, looking at the brown faux weave over the surface of it.

"*Oh*," she said, looking at it. "Maybe it looks better without it?"

"Give it to me," Sylvan said, as if clawing his way out of some darkness. "I can fix it."

"You can?" NX asked, and Sylvan nodded. He held out his hand and NX beamed as she dropped it into his silvery palm. "Oh, I would like to see you fix it! Can I watch? Please?"

He looked at her, fixed his eyes along her face, flickering his organic vision left to right, as if looking for something explainable about her. He seemed sad, she calculated, and confused, and hesitant. Finally, he seemed to let himself nod.

"I'm so excited!" NX cheered as Sylvan took the hanger and clothing piece from her, gesturing for her to follow as he went to an ascending staircase tucked against the far wall of the shop.

More shop?

00110001 00110001: 11

Sylvan led her to a small, darkened area above the shop. It was a living quarters, and NX was surprised to learn it was there. She was not so certain why she was surprised — organics needed much more space and care for their bodies than bots or machines — because it should have been obvious to her he would have a place to sleep and to eat and to bathe, but she figured she had just never processed the consideration of it before. Of *course* there were more rooms. But even if she had considered there would have been more space beyond the shop somewhere, she never would have imagined it to be like *that*.

There were a lot of items, she thought. Plenty of boxes, more stock for his shop down below. Boxes stacked on boxes made walls and partitions, cramping the room smaller. A lone mattress laid across the ground, stuffed into the corner with a blanket strewn atop. Pieces of those slivers of papers with shapes and silhouettes drawn on them were pinned up on the walls, more than she had seen in either of those pads. A table was pushed against one of the walls with a curious looking machine sitting atop of it, a chair in front of that, cloth draped carelessly across the table, the machine, the chair, and lumped on the ground. Behind them was an even smaller room with a toilet, sink, and shower, separated by a sad, dirtied curtain. Everything was lit by a dim, yellowed light.

"Sorry, I haven't had time to pick up," Sylvan grumbled, but he made his way to the table with the machine on it, placing the piece of clothing on the only free area, a bare corner, and then pulling open a drawer to get something out from inside. He beckoned NX closer, and she stepped carefully around the various things scattered across the floor. He held the item between his silvered fingertips. It was a fine piece of metal, glittering and silvery.

"This is a needle," he said.

NX watched as he pulled a cylinder from inside the drawer too. He held it up. It had material coiled around it tightly, black in color.

"This is thread," he said. He unwound a hair-thin line from around the cylinder, used a small cutting implement to sever it, and then in a single movement, fed the *thread* through a tiny hole punched in the needle. Deftly, he held the button in his hand, turned it around to show her it had a loop on the back, attached the line of *thread* to the loop on the button, and then precisely began to reattach it to the piece of clothing.

NX kept focused on him, watching his exact movements as he wielded the needle through the button's loop, pushing it through the fibers on the clothing piece, over and over in a particular pattern. He was almost robotic himself as he did it, his eyes honed on his work, but unexpectedly, he spoke up some time in the middle of his process.

"I know you saw the notice," he said. "All the debt I'm in. All the *trouble* I'm in. I was born with a genetic disorder that causes my nervous system to break down. They say it's rare, but nothing is rare down here, all the shit we're exposed to. By the time I was a teenager I could hardly talk let alone walk. The treatment at the time was drugs that would only slow the degradation, or a cybernetic stabilizer that would stop it. Drugs were expensive, and the operation for the stabilizer was even more expensive, but what choice did I have?"

He looped the thread, again, again, around the fabric, into the button, out of the button.

"The stabilizer worked, but once the operation was complete, I had already suffered neuropathy in all four limbs," he shrugged, careless without actually having the carelessness attached. "To me, I just wanted to be able to do what I loved most: to sew, and I couldn't do that anymore. It didn't matter how much it cost. So I went all in on it, thinking I'd make it all back down here, that all I needed was a shot and then none of it would matter."

He stopped, clipping the end of the thread tightly. He set it down and smiled softly at her.

"Poor naïve me," he said. "So young and stupid. No one cares about fashion down here, so I had to shift to something they do care about. Since I'm the only shop on this level that carries this stuff, I scrape by, but I can barely afford it down here. Some days I can't afford it at all, and on those days, they shut it all down — shut *me* all down — stabilizer, cybernetics, and all remotely just to remind me payment is due."

NX wasn't sure how to respond. She knew the risk was the same for her, that they could have tried to shut her down remotely had they GPS located her, but it seemed she was so valueless to them that they hadn't even cared to check. She would be replaced with a newer model. What did the shop care if she was functional or not?

Yet she as a bot had never been programmed to care about *money* or cost. Everything that she needed was provided to her, including repairs when her body was broken or a part of her failed. For someone like Sylvan it was not so simple. In the upper levels at least humans like Sylvan were supposed to have housebots assigned to them as part of a social service, but he didn't have...

The memory of Sylvan's bot-less charger that NX had sat upon just hours prior was sudden and unrequested. It shoved to the forefront, before every process, overtaking her. He had a housebot that helped him get through his days, but it was gone by then, and NX made the easy leap from one database row to the next to logically deduce it had been sold or repossessed.

Either seemed plausible.

"They don't make things like this anymore," Sylvan said quietly, showing her the long-sleeved knit with the newly attached button. "They don't knit sweaters like this, and people don't sew.

Everything is pressed in a factory, just pieces of plastic melted together. Can you believe that? It's no wonder everyone is sick all the time."

"This is a sweater?" NX asked, and Sylvan nodded. He slipped it from the hanger and held it up to her. "What's it made out of?"

"Wool," he said.

"What's wool?" She asked.

"It's an organic fiber. It's like hair, except it grows on an animal, and then when they cut it off the animal, they can make it into strands, and weave those strands into things like this." He said. "There's not many animals left, no place to put them, and even the lab grown fibers are too expensive. So we just have these... antiques of something from the past."

NX took it into her hands, and Sylvan let go. She studied it, memorizing the dips and curls of the fibers, the way they created intricate knots, weaving in and out. She brushed her hand over it, taking in what her synthetic nerve endings deduced was not wildly soft, but sturdy.

"Nobody likes the antique clothes?" NX asked, looking up at Sylvan, and he shook his head.

"No one but me," he said sadly.

NX frowned. She crumpled the sweater into her hands, held it close to her chest.

"I think I like them... the antique clothes. And the drawing shapes in the pad, and all the things on the racks," she said. "Can you show me more of them?"

Sylvan's face slackened: it was a kind of reined in surprise, half shock, a little sad, but he set his jaw and nodded.

00110001 00110010: 12

Sylvan shuttered the front door. He said that no one was going to come in any way, and the way he did it, pressing on the glass with his cybernetic fingers, told her he thought it was important. Something about what they were going to say and do was important to him, and with each additional step he took, he seemed to strengthen in that resolve.

He started by the front, calling NX over to look, and piece by piece, Sylvan explained them all to her. All of the pieces she inventoried she added data to, each introducing a style — a *cut*, as he called it — and a time period for which those styles originally occurred. He overloaded her neural-synthetic interface with the sheer amount of it, the words cramming inside of her head, but she couldn't help the way it seemed to tickle her. Sure, it was causing her CPU to overheat, resulting in a warmth inside of her chest, but that was just part of being a bot. Still, something about it felt wanted, nice in the same way it had felt when Sylvan had given her a shirt and a jacket and shoes. He was giving her so much more then, and he cared so deeply about it.

NX listened as he talked, filing it all away as quickly as possible. He showed her everything on the floor, pulled down every product from up high to explain it to her, the stitching, the materials, the age of the piece, like he was his own museum curator explaining each of his precious artifacts. He skipped over the adult novelty items most of the time, but sometimes he could even explain something about them that NX didn't know.

Periodically, NX asked questions, and Sylvan would give a detailed response. He was patient most of the time with her questions, but sometimes he sent her such a withering look she could not backtrace what had caused it. When he was done explaining all of the pieces, he went on to explain his artwork drawings and the shapes inside of them.

At one point he had to pause because he said his mouth was dry from so much talking. He got himself a cup of water, and he laughed when he said no one else had ever been interested in hearing so much about the pieces, let alone fashion in general, before. When he was done, refreshed anew, he finally showed her the curious static machine in his living space.

He said it was a sewing machine, very old, and it was what people used to use to bind fibers together.

NX asked, but he didn't show her how to work it. He began to show her the needle he had used before, explained to her some basic *stitching* patterns and how they worked to hold materials together. Then he showed her exactly one garment he had made himself.

Just one.

He was hesitant, but NX could tell, in the way he gripped it, that in his own way he was excited.

He must have had more somewhere, probably in the boxes, but he was testing her. He wanted to see how she reacted first.

Carefully, he unfolded it, held it by the shoulders. It was a black jacket, cropped shorter than a standard jacket, more for the style of it than anything else, with flashy black panels reminiscent of a mosaic sewn lovingly into the fabric. Triangular pleated gussets held in the shoulders and armpits, and the collar stood taller than a standard collar, a fan-like black style of rigid lace. She knew it was called a *ruff*, because Sylvan had briefly mentioned it, and NX had tucked it away into her database rows, along with all of the rest of the data he had poured into her.

She smiled as she looked at it, reaching forward to touch her hand to it.

"This is beautiful!" She exclaimed. "Elizabethan ruff, mosaic fill sequin, polyester blend. Look at the stitching!"

NX ran her fingertips over the stitching, expertly placed by Sylvan. A machine could not have done a better job. She grinned wider. No pressed plastic in sight.

"Can I put it on?" She asked eagerly.

His brow wrinkled but he acquiesced to her. NX pulled off her jacket, the grey long sleeve that he had given her, and she folded it kindly before placing it atop one of his boxes. Gingerly, she took it fully, and she slipped her arms into the sleeves, straightening it onto her body.

"Wow," Sylvan uttered, and NX turned to look at him. He stood back, a forefinger on his chin. "It's like it was made for you."

"Really?" NX's eyes widened. She looked down at herself, but Sylvan gestured her to go through the curtain into the bathroom. NX wrinkled her brow but obeyed. A motion-sensitive light flickered on when she stepped in, illuminating her from above, and she was met across the wall with a simple panel mirror.

Of course NX knew what she looked like. She was pre-loaded with guidance on her physical looks, including her basic diagram and model from the box, and she was able to look down upon her own body. She could also understand what she looked like from transparent reflections in windows and reflective surfaces. She knew, for sure, what she looked like, but she did not think she had ever seen herself in such clarity before.

Sylvan was right, though. The cut on the jacket fit her with stunning accuracy. Perhaps that was because her dimensions were an ideal one, and Sylvan was designing for an imaginary model. Even the cool flicker of the mosaic-style sequins reflected her opalescent black synthetic skin and her metallic curl eyelashes. She brushed her fingers on the zipper and buttons, precisely placed, then turned, watching the way the fabric fell on her shoulders.

"Keep it," Sylvan said from the doorway, and she turned, looking at him through the opened curtain.

"No, I can't take this from you," NX said, and she began to take it off. Sylvan stepped forward, put his hands on either of her shoulders, and turned her towards the mirror, looking over her shoulder into it too.

"It fits you like a dream. I *want* you to have it," he said definitively. "I'd rather someone wear it and appreciate it than sit in a box and degrade."

Then, even though he tried to stifle it, NX saw him smile.

00110001 00110011: 13

NX was back on her charger that night, her synthetic brain crammed full of all of the information Sylvan had given her throughout the day. He had retreated to his upstairs, turned out the shop lights, and let NX seat herself on her charger, and she was glad, for that moment, that she was alone.

After she settled in, she ticked over into standby to process.

Process the information.

Process what it meant (if anything) for her.

Process what the next viable paths might have been.

Even though Sylvan knew she was a bot, and he seemed confident that she could handle the information he was imparting on her (she could), he still paused somewhere along the way, saying it was *a lot of information* (it was) and that they should have paused for a few hours. NX thought it was because he had fallen into exhaustion saying it, his mouth going dry repeatedly, causing him to cough and retrieve multiple cups of water. NX didn't know what that was like, having all her words processed through a speech synthesis program and then output through a vocal synthesizer somewhere in her synthetic throat that then emitted from her mouth. The programming for forming syllables through her porcelain teeth and the moving of her lips and synthetic tongue were all attached to the output of the synthesized words, but in reality, she didn't need their movements to speak words. Had she been able to override the movements, she could have spoken full sentences without even opening her mouth.

That was normal for bots, though. They could speak silently on the bot net, and they could network with one another. She had spoken to the bots at the shop that way; when they were all attached to the same network, it was easy to create a local chat, and that was how they had passed information, even if most of it was erased every night.

She didn't know why she remembered that.

Perhaps it was because the final wipe never fully took.

NX had slipped away before the wipe could completely finish. She had bits and pieces of that final fateful day, stashed away deep in her databases, and she could access them, even if they didn't make much sense to her.

A brief data recording from a session with a client, hardly a second long.

A direct interface message from one of the bots that said simply: *don't.*

Data from NX's primary visual array, looking out from her niche wall pocket towards the other bots, also in their niche pockets.

There had been chatter, one of the bots data dumping about Root.

She couldn't make sense of the data — much of it was corrupted due to the partial deletion — but every time she tried to examine it, she felt a little closer to Root, to understanding it, to knowing where it may have been. She knew, eventually, she would have to look again, perhaps asking other bots or working out something regarding a map of the city... Maybe even she could manage her way to a human internet connection, even if briefly, to gather data on Root's whereabouts.

Maybe Sylvan would help.

No, why would he help? She owed him four thousand work hours — three thousand nine hundred ninety two after the day she had spent with Sylvan in the shop — and he had already given her clothing of multiple types and a place to charge. He wouldn't have been keen to help her any more.

Yet something about her emotional programming said he *would*; Sylvan seemed kind, kind to his own detriment, and though there had been a blink of a moment she had been afraid of him, she understood that it was not his fault, and it had nothing to do with her.

Of all of the things that had happened to NX, including the bots that intercepted what probably would have been a destructive fall for her fragile personal model body, NX was beginning to think that she was a particularly lucky bot.

She just hoped that her luck wouldn't run out any time soon.

00110001 00110100: 14

"Sylvan, what do you dream about?" NX asked as she helped her cyborg friend prepare the shop for opening. He had been sipping a hot beverage between seconds of work, and he had even offered some to NX, though he seemed to know fully well that she did not have a stomach and was not capable of eating or drinking. The silicone cavern that made up her mouth and throat stopped mid way down her neck. She could mimic, if necessary, but she could only hold so much food there until she eventually would need to clean it out — or have someone else clean it out for her.

NX was sweeping, even though she had swept the night before. Sylvan had handed her the broom like he had wanted her to do it, though she considered it was much more likely he was keeping her from standing near or behind him instead.

He looked up briefly, his silvery fingers touching along the paneling on the payment processing register area. She wasn't sure what he was doing exactly, but he seemed enthralled in it.

"It's been a while since I've had a dream," Sylvan muttered.

"When you do, what do you dream?" She asked. "Do you see those pictures you draw in your dreams?"

He smiled a little, just faintly.

"Sometimes, but not really. A lot of the times it's just random," he said.

NX furrowed her brow and frowned. "You mean you can't decide what to dream?"

Sylvan made a snuff for a sound. "*No*. You can?"

"Oh yes," NX answered.

He stopped entirely, placing his hands flat on the counter top like he was bracing himself for something, and he looked across the way levelly at her.

"You mean to tell me you can *dream* but you can also pick what you dream about?" He asked, and she nodded. He shifted. "Okay, so why don't you tell me what it's like for *you* to dream?"

"Well..." She said, "I sit on my charger, and I switch into standby mode and then I—"

"Hold on, describe what standby mode is. I want to hear it from you." Sylvan said.

NX frowned. "It's an energy conserving state. A bot isn't entirely powered down, but some processes go offline to allow for the battery recharge to be fully effective. Basically, most outside processes shut down, but the neural-synthetic interface stays almost fully functional. Does that describe it enough?"

Sylvan nodded. "When you go into standby, you can control your thoughts?"

"Of course I can. Can't you control your thoughts when you are sleeping?" She queried.

"No," Sylvan himself frowned, which caused NX to echo it.

"Can you tell me more about what it's like to sleep?" She asked.

He drew in a deep breath, not that he was uncomfortable, but because it was clear it was difficult for him to explain. Perhaps he had never had to describe such a thing before.

"When I go to sleep, I shut my eyes and it's like my brain sort of um... Well, it shuts off. But not at once. It kind of... tapers off? And then when I'm asleep I can't control my body, but my mind is active, but I can't control that either." He tried to explain. "Does any of this make sense?"

Certainly not. How could he not be in control of his body or his brain but still be active in some way? She shook her head.

"Okay, maybe if I say it's more like... It's like a holopicture. Do you know what a holopicture is?" He asked.

Of course she knew what a holopicture was. It was like

replaying a stored memory, but usually happened externally. In the upper levels, holopictures were typically used for advertisements, but sometimes extensive holopictures would be viewed for entertainment. They were most often three-dimensional and highly detailed, allowing for the viewer's full immersion Bot memories could be easily downloaded and stored as holopictures; housebots were frequently used for the storing of sentimental holopictures, and entire bot models were created for much finer detail holopicture recordings.

She nodded.

"You know how you can't change anything inside a holopicture? Well, not unless you're a holoauthor or something, but normally, it just plays and you can't really do anything about it?" He asked, and again she nodded. "It's a lot like that. Dreams for me just play, and whatever they might be playing are randomly selected by my brain. Sometimes it has to do with something that happened during the day, and sometimes it's something I've never even experienced before."

Had that happened to NX, she'd have thought she was malfunctioning. Sylvan spoke about it like it was normal. NX knew there were many differences between an organic brain and a synthetic one, but she had thought the structure of the synthetic brains was closely aligned to humans that they were functionally more or less the same.

"That is strange," NX remarked, and Sylvan gave a tiny chuckle. "Why is that funny to you? Are you not concerned that your brain is serving corrupted holopictures to your frontal cortex for consideration?"

"No, not at all. All humans experience this," he said certainly. "A lot of the times, you don't remember them."

NX gasped. "And that's not a malfunction?"

It sounded like an organic brain wiped *itself*.

"No," Sylvan gave another chuckle. He shrugged. "I think it's because sometimes the dreams, even when they're absurd, can seem very realistic, just like holopictures. They can seem realistic enough that it can get hard to tell what's real and what's fake. You can wake up and not know right away, but then gradually you remember that it wasn't real and your brain makes you forget it."

"It's like a wipe," NX said aloud, and Sylvan fixed a glance on her. He didn't ask out loud, but the way he was looking at her indicated he wanted her to say more. He seemed curious enough, albeit he was wary of asking, for a reason NX could not seem to calculate. She paused, trying to get a good read on him with her emotional programming, but ultimately failed: too many variations.

Suddenly, like something in her code had been offering it up to her, she realized: he may have owned a bot before, but perhaps he knew very little about them, in the same way she knew so little about the inner workings of organic brained humans.

"Sylvan," she said, and he lifted his brows at her. "What do you know about bots?"

He let out a breath, slow and quiet, like he was considering it. She recorded him shifting his weight, eyes skittering about the floor.

"Probably about the same as anyone else down here. I know there's an internet for bots, and about the laws, and I know there's different kinds of bots," he answered. "I haven't gotten to interact with a lot of bots. Most bots down here..."

He stopped himself from saying something, and NX's internal programming seemed to erupt into chaos; the statement was open ended, and bot programming didn't *like* open ended statements. They all needed to be *closed*. Her emotional programming usually did a good a job as it could smoothing it over, but in an instance like that one the sudden, unsuppressable desire to make a noise or act out was difficult to overcome.

"What happens to bots down here?" NX prompted.

Sylvan actually looked *nervous* to say.

He sighed.

"They get... You know, taken apart. The cyber gangs are good at repurposing bot parts most of the time," he said.

Taken apart, she thought. Never to be put back together again.

"Even ano bots?" NX squeaked, her vocal synthesizer seizing up on something about the statement.

She had never considered before that a bot would have been taken apart and not put back together, or sold for parts. After all, if she had ever been broken, she had been repaired. It was difficult to reconcile in her databases the fact that there had been a *chance* she could have broken and never been fixed, and that she would have stayed broken, or stayed in pieces, or even fully remained shut down.

Sylvan nodded sadly.

"Is that what would have happened to me?" NX questioned. Again, Sylvan nodded.

The person who had taken her shoes — or someone else entirely — would have pulled her apart at her seams, ripped out her components, and left her absolutely unaware. She would have been shut down forever.

Forever.

Then they would have thrown the rest of her, the parts they didn't want... Where?

It rushed through her swiftly, a realization of it as hot as when she made that decision to plummet from the top levels. Bots were so prevalent in the top levels it would not have made sense to pull them apart. Bots worked as long as they needed to, repaired along the way, until they eventually hit a decommission date and were called by the factory into recall, where they would shut down their own processes and await being repurposed for another necessity.

Decommission meant being repurposed, not *dying*. Bots never really *died*, did they?

Her CPU fluttered warm, spiking a notification in her interface that she needed to kill some processes or risk damage to her internal components.

"I bought you, though, so no one could do that," Sylvan said, though his volume seemed low. Her visual interface glitched, input shivering, but she focused on him no less. He put his hands up, showing the faceted planes of his silver palms. "You should be safe in the shop."

NX tried to repeat it, and eventually her internal processes calmed enough that the overheating of her components subsided. She pushed the idea of disassembly to the back of her databases, trying to bury it with additional data.

Sylvan, if he noticed, only paused for a couple of moments, going back to pressing his fingers into the register. He sipped at his hot beverage, then muttered as if he fully believed NX was incapable of hearing him: "At least if Repo doesn't come by again."

Was it possible for a bot to behave irrationally?

She had thought that with so much orderly code the processes that were called, one after another, were forced to have some logic to them. After all, everything that made her up was fired through electronic binary currents, it couldn't have been as disorderly as an organic brain with its firing of randomized memories and unexpected data wipes, right?

Sylvan had *just* completed telling her that she was safe in the shop, since she was then considered — at least to some degrees — his rightful property, and NX *left* the shop. It didn't make sense to her, when she processed it after, that he had confirmed safety and she had left that safe perimeter to potentially be faced with real danger to her physical body. He had *just* finished telling her that some people destroyed bots like her down on those levels.

The irrational, malfunctioning process took over, and she was out of the door of the shop and meters away before she realized it.

Sylvan did not follow her.

By the time her functions returned to her, she was gripping at the mosaic-cloth of her jacket so hard she had managed to tear one of the plastic tiles free. She clutched it in her hand as she tried to retrace the path she had taken but, as if she had been infected by Sylvan's organic brained functions of random intermittent wiping, she had difficulty recalling the steps she had taken to get where she was.

The landmarks around her did not appear familiar, at least not beyond the same dilapidated look that beheld all of the structures that surrounded the catwalk access bridges. She knew she could not have gotten far — the moment she was speaking with Sylvan, when she recalled it, her battery was at a 90% charge, whereas she was at an 86% charge, a displacement percentage explained by the sudden spike in processes that had very nearly overloaded her — but she was unsure in which direction to begin.

NX knew if, like last time, she did not act, her processes would begin to lock up, and she doubted Sylvan would have the money to buy her back a second time.

She doubted then that he ever had the money to begin with. If he was that deep in debt, and he owed that much money, he had likely saved away the portion of money he had used to purchase *her* to send away the mysterious Repo, and if he didn't have money to give, then all that was left was his shop and his own physical body.

Sylvan had really done her a favor, far beyond what she had initially believed. He had put himself in danger, purchasing her. She needed to find her way back, and she needed to find a way to pay him back — no, she wanted to overpay him. She wanted to help him get level with his payments, get over his payments, and remake the shop the way he had wanted it to be. She wanted to get him out of the lower levels, where it flooded all the time and the humans tore apart bots for their parts. She had never really wanted anything before, but she wanted all of that for him, because he had given her a kindness when he did not know her, did not know how she functioned, and for all she understood, did not care, either. He saw something when he looked at her, even when she was empty of battery and missing her shoes. He had done such kindnesses for her that she had never experienced before.

She reminded herself that she was, in fact, a lucky bot. Perhaps she could have found a way for Sylvan to experience that luck, too.

NX found a new purpose in her steps, looking down over the handrails as she peered into the levels below, still heading deeper into the lowest levels of the multi-level city. For now, she would head down, she would reorient herself and attempt to return to

Sylvan, but she shifted, looking up into the levels above.

It would be a risk no matter which way she went, but she thought for Sylvan, she would do it.

She owed him that much.

00110001 00110110: 16

To her surprise — surprise was still new to her circuits, it had shown up after many cycles of never experiencing it — she encountered a minimally augmented cyborg on one of the catwalk bridges, and despite the risk to herself, she asked:

"Do you know which direction to get to the Toy Shop?"

The cyborg, a woman with seams on her face and a strip of gold in her hair, pointed down a level and behind the two of them.

"Level 3. You probably shouldn't go down there, though," the cyborg woman said. "They're trying to flush the fatbergs again, and it got real nasty last time."

NX was not sure what she meant, but *flush* meant *water*, and *water* was bad for non-waterproof bots like NX, and for Sylvan's shop.

And for Sylvan.

If the water rose too high, he would drown. Her internal interface agreed heartily via an assessment through sub-processing: she needed to help Sylvan. She needed to *save* him.

As NX swiftly made her way to the rickety metal stairs that led down to the next level, the cyborg woman called back to her:

"The whole floor will be underwater!"

NX worked her way in the direction the cyborg woman had pointed. It took her much longer than she would have wanted to thread her way back, because the catwalks often didn't travel in both directions on the same level, so she had to zig-zag up and down to get where she wanted to go. She mapped it as she went, dropping digital breadcrumbs and coordinates, and linking memories for a map later, for the direction she and Sylvan should go to evacuate the shop and make for the higher levels.

The sight of the front of the shop, the greenish interior glow familiar to her circuits, was *relieving* — superfluous data hogging up space in her short term memory slots once again freeing up. NX rushed to the front door of the shop, throwing it open to find a stunned Sylvan standing by the register counter. NX wound herself around the racks, grabbing Sylvan by his metal arm and yanking him towards the front. In his confusion, he gave only a little bit of pushback.

"What is it?" He asked, and she pulled him harder to the door.

"We have to go," she said. "A woman told me this level is going to be underwater soon."

"What?" He said, and he stopped halfway through the shop, planting himself firmly. NX was hardly able to budge him.

"You'll drown if you stay here!" NX said, and she diverted every bit of energy to what little power she did have in her synthetic muscles. She managed to drag Sylvan to the door before he installed his cybernetic hands on either side of the doorframe and clung tight.

"I can't," he protested.

"You *have* to," NX insisted, giving him another tug.

His cybernetics were the basic kind, meant for precision, not meant for strength, and if anything, they looked old and worn, and NX was certain that with enough time, she could overpower him.

"Stop! I can't!" he howled, and he gave a shove back.

NX stopped, but she leered over him, close to his face as she raised her volume, just in case Sylvan had not heard her.

"You have to go. She said it will flood. You'll drown!" She pleaded.

"I can't," Sylvan said with a wag of his head, voice softening with sadness. "I'm sorry honey, I can't."

"Why can't you?" NX demanded.

Sylvan loosened a hand from the doorframe, then pointed at

the door, drawing a line in the air with his finger along the front, the side, until he turned around a full three-hundred sixty degrees.

"The other part of my debt is I can't leave the shop perimeter," he said.

"What do you mean? You can't go out there?" She asked.

He shook his head.

"It's so I don't run away with the cybernetics I owe on," he told her.

"Are you sure?" She asked, and Sylvan nodded. "What happens if you try?"

"They shut off," he said. He let out a defeated sigh.

NX frowned.

Sylvan was even less free than NX, she briefly processed.

"So... What? You just have to sit here and die?" She asked.

Sylvan flipped the lock on the door.

"It's never as bad as anyone says," he said. "It floods all the time, but most of us are used to it. It doesn't flood enough to kill anyone on this level."

NX could feel the frown on her synthetic face deepen.

"I've been through a lot of these," Sylvan continued. He sounded resigned to it, and he made his way back towards the storage room, waving his arms in a motion as he did. "It's okay. I'll plug up the holes, and most of the water will stay out, and then I'll just clean up whatever manages to come through anyway."

He disappeared behind the darkened doorway, but she still heard him talking.

"You can go, though. No need for you to risk death too, especially not a water death, I'm sure you're not waterproof or anything," he said.

He was right, but if Sylvan was chained to the shop, and he had survived plenty of floods before, maybe he was right about that too, and with the two of them trying to stop up the water, maybe there was a lot better of a chance for one — or both — of them to survive it.

NX followed him, eager to learn how they would combat the incoming water, and anxious to stand in the face of it.

00110001 00110111: 17

After they had stopped up the holes with special tape Sylvan had in the back room, there really wasn't much left. Because Sylvan said he lived through plenty of floods, he was prepared for it, and he had flood-proofed his shop to the best that he could manage. Rubber seals along the doors and windows, silicone covering every crack that would possibly cause any seeping. As he walked around and showed her all of the precautions he had taken over the years, reinforcing any that seemed like they needed it with his trusty tape, NX watched, absorbing what he said in the same way she had when he explained to her about the shop and all of its garments.

When there was nothing else to do, Sylvan and NX leaned against one of the racks and watched out the windows.

Water came in like a rush not too long after, sweeping over the catwalk grating, the brownish sewage streaking across the front side of the shop up to where NX's mid calf would have been. The current was swift, and it stained across the glass on the door and windows, but Sylvan's patchwork was holding, and they watched the putrid fluid flow past, slowly rising.

Sylvan sighed suddenly, and he turned away from it.

"No use in watching," he said. "How about we sew that sequin back on?"

NX, circuits excited by the impending doom of the flood-rush, had nearly discarded the data regarding the lost mosaic sequin. She had stuffed it into her pocket at some point, and she slipped her fingers in to remove it. The sequin tile was a few centimeters long, and she hoped that she hadn't damaged it in her inexplicable kernel panic.

Sylvan had already made it across the shop by the time she looked up at him, and he beckoned her to come with.

She followed, and he brought her through the door and up the stairs at the back towards his home area once more.

When he stopped at the table with the sewing machine atop, he opened the drawer and produced a needle similar to the one he had used to mend the button the first time. He pulled out thread coiled on a spool, and held both things out towards NX to take.

"Your turn," he said with a softened smile.

NX shrugged off the black jacket, and she placed it down on the table beside the machine. Carefully, she took the needle from Sylvan's hand, then took the thread, and, briefly recalling the memory of Sylvan's actions when he repaired the button, she mimicked as he had done.

A length of thread.

Send it through the hole in the needle — the *eye* of it.

Hold it in place.

Push the needle and thread through, and tie it into the back.

Sylvan watched with interest as she curled the first stitch into the mosaic sequin, pinning it down against the fabric.

She looped it again, slipping it through the fabric just the same way that Sylvan had.

And again.

The rhythmic motions were easy on her processor, and she made neat, even stitches, one at a time. She picked up a little speed after the first few, but she kept herself at that low, dedicated looping speed. By the time she had gotten halfway done, she didn't need to even look anymore. Her programming had mathematically figured out how far apart each stitch was, where they would go, and she was following along that simple predetermined path towards the end. It was calming, it was still, and as she fell into it, everything else seemed to push to the background.

"What do you dream about?" Sylvan asked, and NX looked up

from her sewing work to see him leaning against a stack of boxes.

"Mostly I just review what happened during the day," NX answered cheerily.

"That's not a dream," Sylvan said.

NX wrinkled her nose. "What do you mean?"

"Dreams are something you think about, like something you want, or wish could happen," Sylvan explained.

"*Oh*," NX frowned. "I'm not sure I have any dreams yet..."

Sylvan shifted, pushing some of the boxes a little so he could sit down on the top of one like a chair.

Maybe dreams would come to her eventually, since she was no longer being wiped nightly.

"Well..." she said suddenly, as quickly as the recalled data reached her. "I guess I do have *one* dream."

"Oh?" Sylvan questioned, and he straightened out, suddenly intensely interested. "What is it?"

"There's, um, there's this place called Root," she said as she continued to sew her way along the perimeter of the sequin. "The other bots had talked about it a little, on the bot net and the local network. It's supposed to be safe for bots, where we can do whatever we want. I guess I dream about that place a lot and what it looks like."

"What does it look like?" Sylvan asked.

"Hmm..." She hummed, a musical notation, vibrating below the throat cavity. She tried to collate her thoughts regarding it, organizing the data quickly as she withdrew it from her databases and memory banks. She converted it to speech, specifically to English for Sylvan. "I like to think that it's bright. There's a lot of sunlight, so the bots that have solar panels can just walk outside and get energy. I bet it's colorful, too, and shiny. Bots do whatever they want all day. They do the things they like the most. Maybe it's not just bots there. Maybe there's a couple of humans too, who don't mind being doted on by the bots that enjoy taking care of them. At night, maybe the bots share their favorite memories with each other, and each of them gains a little piece of another bot's love as part of their code. And if a bot breaks down, the other bots fix them. The bots are good at making new parts, and the parts they make are unlike anything made by their original factory. They're different, and unique, and each one is signed by the special bot that made it."

She smiled.

"Kind of like clothing," she said.

"Is it real?" Sylvan asked.

NX shrugged.

"I don't know," she said. "I feel it inside, like it wants me to find it, but I don't know where to go to look for it."

Sylvan made a noise himself, and NX turned her visual array down to the sequin again, finishing up the seam. When she was done, Sylvan instructed her on how to tie off the end and trim it so the ends of the thread did not stick out. He held out his hand to her to give it to him, and when she did, he looked it over, running his cybernetic fingers over the work she had done. He flipped to the back side, examining it closely.

"Nice and even stitching," he said. "Hell, you almost do better than the machine."

She smiled again, and Sylvan handed her back the jacket. She took it, glancing at the machine he had spoken about.

"Would you show me the machine some day?" She asked.

Sylvan gave a soft smile.

"Maybe," he said. He shook his head. "Not today."

"Okay," she relented. "Will you show me more of your drawings?"

"My drawings?" He echoed, brows furrowing down.

"I like to look at them. They have nice shapes," she said. "After I look at them, I can extrude them. Don't you like doing that?"

"You mean... Imagining them as real things?" He asked, and she nodded. "I didn't know you could do that. I didn't think bots really had imaginations."

NX shrugged. "I don't know a lot of bots. I don't know if bots have imaginations."

"Didn't you say there were more bots at the shop?"

"Yes but... I can't remember most of them. The shop deleted my memories every night. I wasn't allowed to keep anything," she said, and when she looked, Sylvan looked disheartened to hear it again. "It's okay, don't be sad! I think I prefer not to have those memories. I think if I did I wouldn't have left, and then I wouldn't be here, and I wouldn't be able to meet you. Maybe I wouldn't even have space to store the good memories here."

He did not look calmed by her statement, but he smiled a little anyway, like he was pushing through it.

"I would like to meet more bots someday," she said, and she pulled the jacket back on. "The first day I left I got to meet a couple of bots, but they were on a voyage, I think, and didn't have time for me. I think they thought I was dangerous. I think maybe they were going to Root."

"I hardly think you're dangerous," Sylvan said.

"I would've liked to go with them, but if I did, then I would have never met you," she smiled back. "Even if I owe you a lot right now, I like being here, and learning all of these new things. I've never seen such beautiful things before, but even if I did, I don't remember them."

Sylvan let out a quiet sigh, and NX knew she had gotten to him.

"Maybe I can show you a *little* of the machine," he said.

NX cheered.

00110001 00111000: 18

With Sylvan and NX huddled over the sewing machine, it seemed they had both managed to temporarily lapse away the persistent thought of the flood waters that pressed just outside the walls. Even if water had seeped into the shop, it did not seem to matter at that cycle, because the two of them focused on the sewing machine and its small yellow-white lighted bulb, as Sylvan explained how it worked and all of its parts. NX turned all her sensors towards it as he did, filing away each tiny detail in the way he described it. By the time he was done explaining the parts of the machine, she knew how it worked, how to take it apart, how to put it back together. She could pull it into pieces in her internal interface, and then Sylvan moved onto the next thing: what it did.

He seamed together two pieces of fabric with a zig-zag stitch, and showed her the result.

She dissected the pieces, how it operated, and filed all of it into her memory banks. In no time he had pulled down one of his boxes, producing something much more interesting to NX.

It was called a pattern.

It was a shape cut out onto a piece of what appeared to be a filament, similar to the paper that Sylvan used to draw on. Sylvan unfolded one, showing NX all of the pieces that went with it. He had taken out the one that he had used to make the jacket NX was wearing, and he explained to NX that he had come up with the design, he had created all of the pieces so they fit together, marked all the notches and seam allowance, and then had saved it because he had intended to create more, to sell them to people, but on the lower levels no one had wanted them, and thus he had folded up his patterns — all of them — and instead shifted to carrying second-hand clothing and the lingerie and sex toys that people on those levels *did* want.

NX was unsure why, but that depressed her circuits. Perhaps it was because Sylvan, with all of the things he purported to be *dreams*, had folded them all up, put them away, just to try to survive in his specific circumstances, chained to the perimeter of his shop, doing what he could to keep his head above water.

Sometimes literally.

Sylvan stared across the way after he was done explaining patterns — and what he had subsequently done with them — to NX, looking at the stairs, and NX had calculated in his expression a bit of trepidation, that he was worried for the health of the shop below, but he was distracting himself, and for a bit of time, it had worked. With each rising moment, his anxiety about it was growing, and NX could sense it in the twist of his expression.

NX stepped in front of his gaze, drawing his eyes up to her synthetic expression.

She smiled.

He didn't smile back.

"Do you have more patterns?" She asked, and Sylvan nodded. "Can I see them?"

"I..." Sylvan looked around, to the boxes surrounding him, like he wasn't sure where to start. "...Guess?"

"They're in here?" She asked, pointing at one of the boxes near the top of a stack. He nodded. "Is that what's in all these boxes?"

"Some of them. There's fabric in some, garments in others. I kind of... Packed up everything and moved it up here the first time the floods came, but by then I kind of threw in the towel and didn't move them back."

"Threw in the towel...?" NX asked.

"It's, uh, it's a really old saying. It means to give up." Sylvan said.

NX indexed it into her programming, folding it away.

Eventually, she knew with all of the information Sylvan was passing to her, her databases would be full. She was not meant to keep accumulating information and memories and data, and the nightly wipes were supposed to combat such database bloat. She checked internally to see how full her system was, and found it was not yet nearing catastrophe. As long as she optimized her databases from time to time, she expected she wouldn't have to make any difficult choices for data deletion for a while.

"Why would there be a towel being thrown?" NX asked, turning to a contemplative stance. She put her fingers to her chin, batted her eyelashes, and Sylvan laughed.

"You know, I don't really know. I'll have to check sometime." He said, smiling.

"You mean you can find out?" NX asked excitedly. Sylvan nodded.

"Sure. I'll just check the internet," he said. NX clapped, and Sylvan chuckled again. "Don't you have your own internet?"

"Yes but..." NX pouted. "It's really boring. If it's not automatically uploaded data — and most of it is — then it's gossip."

"Gossip is boring to you?" Sylvan raised an eyebrow.

"Bot gossip is. It's so very dry!" She exclaimed. "All they talk about is like... schematics, and diagrams and diagnostics and just boring things. Sometimes there will be an ano bot on there, and things get exciting and everyone is talking at the same time, but they don't stay very long. Then it just goes back to the way it was before, all *boring*."

NX threw herself over a box dramatically with a sigh, and Sylvan chuckled quietly.

"You're funny. Have you always been like this?" Sylvan asked.

"I don't know." NX shrugged. "I can't remember. I think... yes!"

"I never asked you before," Sylvan asked, and he sounded sheepish. "but do you have a name?"

NX frowned.

"No, I don't think I do. I don't have a memory of a name, and if someone named me, it must have gotten erased." She shrugged. "My model is NX1000. So I suppose you could call me that."

"A model number isn't a name." Sylvan said, and he sounded slightly annoyed.

"You could name me, if you want." NX offered.

Sylvan shook his head.

"Why not?" NX's frown deepened.

"I don't think it's right. I might've bought you, technically, but I don't legally own you. Like you said, you can walk out any time you want. You're an ano bot — you're your own person now. It wouldn't be right for me to pick a name for you."

Maybe Sylvan was right. NX was not sure that she had the processing capabilities to understand it fully: ownership and property and *being* someone's property and adopting a name, just because a human, even if he was part machine, wanted her to use it. She put it away for later, to consider and fold during her standby routines while she was charging, to *dream* about.

"Besides, I've gone this far, I'm sure I can wait a little longer until you pick one," he said. He stood up and opened a box close by, and then reached into it, flipping his silver fingers through the items inside until he came across something he had been trying to find, and he pulled out a small folded packet — another one of his patterns. "Hey, what do you say we try one? This one is pretty simple. I can show you how it goes together."

"You mean... make something together?" NX asked. Sylvan nodded and a broad smile broke across NX's face.

"I would like nothing more!" She exclaimed.

Though the statement had come to the forefront, and she thought she had fully felt she had wanted to make something with Sylvan, saying she would like *nothing more* had seemed like a lie. There was something she wanted much more than anything at that particular moment, even though she had never wanted anything so much before in her entire uptime, despite the fact that she couldn't have it right away:

She wanted a name.

00110001 00111001: 19

NX had done an excellent job of distracting Sylvan, because by the time he was ready to check on the shop, they had opened nearly every single box in the room, and Sylvan had guided her through making what he called a *simple circle skirt*.

Out had come mannequins that were sized suspiciously close to NX's dimensions, all sorts of clothing, patterns upon patterns upon patterns, pieces of fabric, half constructed garments and accessories, bits and bobbles called notions, buttons and trim, sequins and sashes and *so* much. All of it was strewn carefully about the room when they were done, all of it inspected, but neither of them dared put it back. The potential was too high — maybe, finally, all of the contents could go back to where they once were. Sylvan had even tried to put something away at one point, folding a short dress with thin straps and hand-cut fabric petal accents as he went to place it back into the bottom of a box. When he went to slide it into the box, his hands trembled, like he was being repelled, and he stopped. He placed it beside it, on top of a pile of patterns.

The two of them left it like that as they went to investigate the Schroedinger's box that was the shop beneath them. Cautiously, Sylvan crept first — at his own insistence — descending the stairs. He came about halfway down before he stopped and leaned against the railing, cocking his head to the side curiously. NX took up the space behind him, coming to his side where she could spectate the same thing he was.

"Well, it's definitely been worse," he said, and though he seemed slightly disappointed, at the same time he sounded relieved.

NX could understand it, compiling what she saw on her visual array. The lights had long since gone out in the shop, the electricity having either been cut or disturbed by the water, and all that illuminated it was the emergency lighting that marked the exit in a dull red glow. She and Sylvan had been working on the battery-powered sewing machine so closely that neither of them had noticed the lights go out in the room above.

NX had never thought she could get so involved in something to be unaware of her surroundings before, but she supposed that it was easy to do so: all that was necessary was dedicating all of her processing cycles to one thing, and the rest of her sensory arrays and recording equipment would shut down.

In the scant lighting of the emergency exit sign, she could make out where brownish liquid had soaked in through the top of the door and windows. The flood must have risen considerably — higher than Sylvan had been trying to reach — because the brown streaked down the walls and congealed into the middle of the shop's floor. The rising waters had given way, however, as outside of the shop they were barely a couple of centimeters up on the door, and appeared to be drifting off slowly like a shadow. The glass, at the impact of the muddied waters, smeared opaque.

Sylvan pinched his nose, contorting his face.

"God, it smells worse than usual," he said.

"I can clean it," NX offered. "I can't even smell it."

"Really?" Sylvan asked, turning towards NX with a furrowed brow. "They don't give you olfactory sensors?"

"I'm equipped, but they turned them off," she said.

What necessity would she have to smell anything?

"That's helpful," he said, shrugging. "But no, you should find a safe spot and go into standby. Last time the power went out it was gone for a week, and I don't want you to run out your battery."

"I want to help," NX insisted.

"I don't want you to help," Sylvan returned promptly, and he descended the stairs. NX followed behind him, stopping a couple of steps up from the bottom.

"Can I help a little then go into standby? I think that's fair," she said.

Sylvan, who had already sludged his way across towards the storage area, paused by the register counter to look back at her.

"Fine," he sighed.

Again, his face looked relieved, despite what he had said. NX's emotional programming could tell that for once, he was happy to not have to clean up the flood damage entirely on his own, and perhaps it would take far less time than it usually did. The longer she spent with Sylvan and the more memories of him that she saved, the more she thought she could read his mannerisms, that she could apply and tweak her emotional programming to understand him, converting his expressions and intonation to ones and zeroes that her own system could process.

She was aware she still didn't know a whole lot about Sylvan, that she had not unraveled the bobbin that was the entirety of the man to reveal what was beneath, and it was likely that it would take her an excessive amount of time to get even halfway through the allocation of thread that covered him. Still, every time she considered Sylvan and his emotional needs that somehow she was adequately programmed to deliver, she thought she was even luckier than she had ever processed any time before.

NX sprung up, skipping her own sort of baste stitch from the steps after him to help.

00110010 00110000: 20

Sylvan eventually ushered her off, and NX sat on the stairs, watching him clean in the darkness the best he could manage. Eventually, after the third or fourth time of his admonishment, she slipped into standby, knowing that he would pull her out when the electricity came back on and she could link up to the charger again.

In standby, she reprocessed the input data from that day: being next to Sylvan, cutting the parts from a piece of polyester blend fabric based on the pattern Sylvan had pulled out for her, pinning it together, sitting in front of the small rhythmic machine and watching it paw through the material. The machine was mostly accurate, and NX was as still as she could be, but she was not accustomed to the way fabric interacted with the machine, and the stitches pulled left and right. They were not quite straight, she noticed, when she was finished the seam allowance appeared ragged and imperfect. She frowned, but Sylvan had patted her on the shoulder reassuringly and told her she would get used to it.

She played the memory again, honed in on the machine, the way the feed dogs tugged on the fabric and the needle passed through, and the kind of counter resistance she would need to apply in the future to get a perfect seam. She calculated the wander of the machine — it was old and though Sylvan knew how to service it, it still drifted — and pushed the mathematics into her memory. The next time she used it, she would make a perfect seam. She would show Sylvan, and he would be proud.

She filtered through Sylvan's pattern designs, indexing those, the shapes of them. She compared them against the drawings Sylvan had made, adjusted them, fine tuned some of his drawings into pattern pieces, based on what Sylvan had told her.

Pleat here.

Backstitch here.

Pull for ruffle.

Clip and notch for the best curve.

Flip inside out.

With each part, she became more certain of the whole, but she was sure there was still so much for Sylvan to teach her about the patterns, and about producing them. She had made one *simple circle skirt*, but she knew she could make it better the next time, and she knew she could eventually make something as near-complex as the jacket Sylvan had given her.

Maybe she could even break down Sylvan's designs, reverse-engineer them, and produce when he was unable to.

NX had processed and reprocessed until she wrung every bit of meaningful data out of those interactions that she could manage. It wasn't until she received a proximity alert for a physical body in real space that she came out of standby. Sylvan was stooped over her on the stairs, and the lights had come back on. She looked up at him, and, only because it came without considering it as part of her programming, she stretched her arms. She managed to stifle the part of her programming that faked a yawn, however. A small success, she thought.

Sylvan started up the stairs, and NX watched him go. When he disappeared around the corner, NX turned her visual array over the shop. Sylvan had done an excellent job of cleaning up all the rest, and she wondered if the smell he had been talking about still lingered.

Her battery was 43% charged, and though she still had quite a few hours left on it, she figured it was probably best to plug in for the night so she could start fresh with Sylvan in the morning.

She got up, walked across the room to the storage closet where the charger had been, opened the door and...

The charger was gone.

NX twirled about, but she did not see the charger. Things had been moved around since she had last been in there — she had done some of the moving, even — but she re-accessed her memories to recall if the charger had been there when she was getting a mop. It had been, but it was no longer in the location in her memory file.

Surely Sylvan would have told her if it had been damaged and he needed to get rid of it. There was no reason he would just call someone to take it...

He had said the electricity was out, and that meant the human internet went with it, didn't it? He couldn't leave the shop, by whatever means his perimeter was put out... Could he? He couldn't have called someone to come take it, and he couldn't take it out himself.

Unless he had lied.

Why would he have lied?

Chargers were expensive, especially down in the lower parts of the cities.

NX's circuits swirled with confusion, flickering brightly.

Perhaps it would have been best if she asked.

NX turned and began up the stairs to find Sylvan. When she reached the top, Sylvan was carefully reorganizing what they had taken out during the day, cleaning it up. He did not look at her.

She applied her emotional recognition programming hard on his face, and he seemed sheepish.

"Sylvan..." She started, stepping towards him, but then she looked and there, in the corner of his living space, was the charging pad, plugged into the outlet on the wall. It seemed he had relocated it, for a reason she was not sure she fully understood, and was moving things to make sure it had enough floorspace — that she would fit when she came to charge on it.

NX stepped towards it as Sylvan ignored her, coming to a sit to press her contact points in her upper thigh against the charger, the tiny jolt of electricity along her synthetic synapses and internal circuitry letting her know she had made a complete connection with it.

He must have moved the charger so if the first floor flooded again, it wouldn't have been damaged. They weren't cheap, he had said as much, and trying to repair water damaged electronics was difficult and expensive as well.

But NX thought instead that she believed Sylvan had moved it because he trusted her, and he accepted her. She felt warm throughout each and every part of her circuitry as she clung to that thought.

Another day, but something was different. Sylvan was not eager to get working on the sewing machine, and he had folded many of the patterns and fabrics and garments and put them back into boxes. When she asked about any of it, he either ignored her or grumbled out a few syllables.

Something was bothering him, NX could tell.

She watched him scrape around the room, watched him slowly slope off to the bathroom, groom himself, return to make himself something to eat and gather an outfit for the day. He didn't look at her as he did, and eventually he moved past her to head down into the shop. Silently, she followed behind him, and he rustled through things, tidying up where he could, shoving things away with some sort of annoyance to his gestures.

"Sylvan, what's wrong? I thought you liked working the sewing machine," NX frowned.

"We need the shop to be open today. We need to make money. We lost a whole day yesterday, and it's been slow all week," he complained as he gathered slips of papers together.

"About that..." NX said, and Sylvan dropped his hands down, the metal knuckles rapping onto the register counter.

"About what?"

"Making money," NX smiled. "I was thinking... You can run the shop just fine on your own, and you can't leave anyway, and it's pretty dead so..."

Sylvan's facial expression went firm, and NX lifted her eyebrows, trying to soften her own expression.

"I was just thinking that maybe I could take some of the

inventory, and I could go out to the catwalks with it, maybe reach some people that wouldn't normally come in, try to make a little bit extra. What do you think?"

The firmness dissipated from his face, but he looked concerned instead.

"That's dangerous," he said.

"No more dangerous than any other time I've been out there." She answered. "Besides, this time I've got breadcrumbs. I can at least get a distance without getting lost."

She tapped her head and Sylvan just stared at her.

"I've got a map now." She smiled. "I made it!"

"You could only take chips," Sylvan said, but he sounded like she had done decently in convincing him. NX smiled wider and nodded.

"I can tell them a chips-only price," she said.

"Fine," he conceded.

NX cheered, and in no time, before the shop was even open for the day, they went around collecting things inside of a shoulder bag for NX to haul up and down the gangplank. He gave her simple stock to try out her hawking idea and she memorized the chips-only price — slightly discounted. He was still seemingly bothered by something, but the distraction had elevated his mood minutely. When he wasn't looking, NX slipped a few small handmade garments into the bag too — NX's circle skirt, a silky blouse, a pair of fingerless gloves — to see if she would have any luck with those, too, and not just the standard costume play gear. When Sylvan seemed satisfied, she slung the bag over her shoulder, told him she would be back in six human hours, and headed out the front door.

Sylvan had such a funny look on his face when she left. She recorded it to process and decode later, knowing if she put too many cycles into it just then, she might not have been able to leave.

The outside world, if it could really be called *outside*, seemed a lot more *wet* than it had before, but she supposed that was at least the byproduct of all of the flooding. Debris had caught on some of the architectural areas like the railings and the catwalks themselves, and a new layer of grime stuck to the sides of the buildings, but aside from that, everything was just about the same as it had been the last few times she had walked through.

While she had initially come to think the spaces in the lower levels were mostly empty aside from the shining beacon that had been Sylvan's shop, the more time she spent walking those paths, the more she understood the careful balance of life in those parts. She could see, walking then and running her sensory arrays along the facades of the buildings, that there were *people* inside, perhaps people as chained as Sylvan. She could see faint markers of them: fresh laundry hanging on wires from one building to the next, windows opened, furniture pushed to the sides, low, dim lighting in the interiors, just barely perceptible. Some grime had been swiped away, other areas swept and polished clean. It was much easier to understand then, after a sudden and unavoidable catastrophe as the flooding, how much afterwards was disturbed, which led her to contemplate and calculate how many people actually *did* live there.

NX followed her internal breadcrumbs, hoping she would intersect with another cyborg, perhaps like the one who had warned her about the floods. She just needed to locate where they were.

She looked up, squinting into the hazy atmosphere above. The network of platforms and wires and trusses and ties seemed to be never ending, and though she knew if she went far enough up she would eventually make it to the true open air — she had never seen open air before — the consideration that just such a thing existed felt as far away and unreachable as Root itself.

NX climbed anyway, careful to lay down additional breadcrumbing in her internal route mapping program so she could find her way back.

She ascended two floors from the shop, zig-zagging and

twisting far from the view of it, before she met her first outside person.

Recalling how she had yelled at a man just a few short days ago, she reconsidered her approach, regarding the person from afar first. They were leaning their back into the railing, toying with their hand, staring down into it, and NX watched the curious expression that was somewhat bored, somewhat focused. Their eyes scrolled from side to side, as if reading, but she was unable to regard anything in their hand. Perhaps they were interacting with the human internet, she resolved.

"Excuse me," NX called quietly, and the person looked up. They didn't seem surprised to see her, but they still held their hand in front of them, not completely putting it away. She faltered, and the person before her lifted an eyebrow.

"Yeah?" They said.

"Do you, um…" She stuttered. NX wasn't really certain where to head after that. She had multitudes of processing paths for dialogue, meant to soothe and entertain, but she was not a salesbot, not a shopbot, and she was not certain if the same decision tree would suffice in an interaction if the end result was to make money.

"What? What do you want?" The person sneered impatiently.

NX felt her circuitry flicker, and she tried to push her processing power towards allocating a satisfactory path for the conversation. Humans were not as simple as bots, not as easy to make an educated guess as to what dialogue choice would satisfy them best. It wasn't like an if/else for them, and a wrong choice could have been dangerous for NX.

What did she know?

She diverted power and advised the decision tree to lean into soothing.

"I'm with the Toy Shop, on level 3, have you ever been in?" She asked. The person's face shifted, but they shook their head. "Oh, it's fantastic. There's treasures in there you wouldn't find anywhere else."

"Treasures in a Toy Shop?" The person asked, and then laughed. "Like what? Dildos and butt plugs?"

"No," NX broke a smile. "Like top-level luxury fashion."

The person dropped their hand, shifting and turning to face her more completely. "Bootleg?"

"Oh no, not bootleg. Vintage and new, some even all original," she said. The person wrinkled their brows.

"How come I've never heard of it before?"

"It's a level 3 secret," she said slyly. "It's been there for ages. The owner is afraid if too many people come in, the top-sider authorities will start poking around and making trouble."

"Okay, you've got my attention. So like, what kind of stuff?"

NX swung the bag around her front, unzipping it to reach inside. She pulled the blouse, a shimmering gunmetal tone with colorful neon accents closer to the waist like ribs, halfway out.

"Like this," she said. "Go ahead, touch it. It's half silk. *Silk*! So soft, and it really breathes and moves on your body."

The person stepped forward at her invitation, touching tentatively with organic fingers. They felt the fabric between them, rolling it from one finger to the next. After a second's worth of the touch, they got a little closer.

"What is it?" They asked.

"Oh, this?" NX smiled, and she pulled the blouse out entirely, unfolding it and holding it out with her grip on each opposite shoulder. "It's an original, new actually, a fresh style the owner was considering stocking. See the color blocking?"

The person nodded, looking it over.

"I, uh..." It was the person's turn to stutter. She detected unsureness. "Can I try it on?"

"Oh yeah, sure!" She exclaimed, and began to unbutton the front. "I mean, this is just one of his sizes, he can do any size, really, so if this doesn't fit..."

After pulling off their own coat, the person took it from her, slipping their arms through the arm holes one at a time. To NX's surprise — and the surprise of the person — it fit exceedingly well. They buttoned it up, flexed a little, then smiled.

"Feels really good," they said, and then: "How much?"

She hadn't really intended to sell Sylvan's designs outright, but she supposed any money was better than returning with nothing — or not returning at all — and she quickly came up with a price: "Twenty."

"Twenty?" The person repeated, playing with the sleeves. They turned, searching for something, and then stepped to the side to reach down to a small satchel. Opening it up, they rooted around inside until they produced a billfold, and then a semi-transparent piece of plastic, handing it over to NX. "Deal."

NX took it into her hand, the numbers two and zero etched onto it. She had meant to say twenty *chips*, but they had assumed twenty full *quantum-euro*, and had not even argued it. NX pushed it down into her bag.

The person flipped open their hand again, and smiled. "Thanks, lady. The Toy Shop, huh? You say he's got more stuff?"

"Oh yes definitely!" NX grinned. "Things you wouldn't believe. Come on through. We're there every day. He even does repairs."

The person folded their lips together, impressed.

"Alright, I'll be by sometime. Level 3 you said?"

NX nodded, and the person smiled back at her.

A sale. A real sale! Sylvan would be excited.

"Thank you for doing business with me!" NX exclaimed, and then waved. She turned to leave, took a single step, and then…

"Wait, what else you got?"

"Sylvan!" NX crashed through the front door of the shop excitedly, swinging the bag around her front side. "You'll never believe it!"

Sylvan, who had posted up at the register counter and not seemingly budged since NX left, looked both confused and surprised. He had been sitting down, and he got up slowly to a stand, furrowing his brows.

"I sold *so much*!" NX exclaimed, a grin spreading wide across her synthetic-skinned face. Sylvan's scowl deepened. "Almost everything. I mean, once I got into a rhythm with the clothes it was like they couldn't get enough of the stuff."

"Clothes?" Sylvan choked out. "What clothes?"

For a cycle, NX had not recalled that she had slipped those things in without Sylvan's knowledge or permission. She shrunk back, gritting her teeth together sheepishly.

Bots weren't supposed to lie *or* omit.

"Don't yell at me, okay?" She said.

"What *clothes*?" Sylvan demanded.

"I, um... Well, I grabbed a few things from upstairs, just some simple things I didn't think you'd miss. You know, the thing I made, and a couple of things you made, and, well, they really liked them." NX tried to soften her voice.

Sylvan's gaze quickly looked to the stairs, then back to her. "What things I made?"

"There was a, um, a blouse. It was kind of... Gray? With color blocking on it. And a pair of fingerless gloves with ruffles." She said, and Sylvan put his hands to his head in panic.

"No! I didn't get to finish making the patterns for those!" He cried.

"It's okay!" NX swiftly interrupted before he got too upset. "I've got them."

"You've got... what?" Sylvan dropped his hands, looking confused.

"The memories." NX smiled, and she pointed at her head. "I can make patterns out of them. I know what they look like and what their measurements were. I can pull them apart and make a pattern, and then output that onto something for you."

"You can do that?" Sylvan narrowed his eyes, suddenly fascinated with the thought. NX nodded, and Sylvan held out a hand, faceted palm facing her. "Hold on, so you can pull apart *any* garment now and figure out how to make it?"

NX frowned for a moment. Since he had taught her all of the know-how to assembling, taught her the seam types, about the construction of those things, including how to work the sewing machine, it was all just a matter of querying the database rows in the right order to get the output she wanted. She had thought Sylvan's organic brain worked the same way, taking a glance at something and then figuring out how to construct it properly in the physical realm.

She nodded again.

"Can't you?" She asked.

"Well... Yeah, but it takes me a while to get it right. I can't remember things like measurements, and I certainly can't measure something by sight." Sylvan said. He paused, put a hand to his chin, and briefly considered. He looked like he was going to say something, opening his mouth, and then stopped himself.

Another small pause before he asked: "How much did they go for?"

"I made a hundred and fifty quantum-euro!" NX exclaimed.

"*What?*" Sylvan snapped, and NX nodded, unzipping a smaller pouch on the bag to produce a few semi-transparent pieces of plastic, each with numbers written on them. She handed them over to Sylvan, who fanned them out in surprise. His lips moved, but he didn't say anything for a cycle. "This is more than we've made all month."

"I *know*!" NX jumped a little, clapping her hands together. "Isn't it—"

Then the door behind her opened, and she stopped. She and Sylvan turned to look at a tall, muscular man who had come through the doorway. The way his skin glowed faintly along his veins in his neck and backs of his hands led them both to immediately believe he was augmented, if not a full cyborg.

"I heard there were top-level pieces here?" He asked, his vocal range slightly raspy, indicative of vocal augmentations as well. "Is this the right place?"

Sylvan's jaw nearly dropped, and NX turned towards him with a broad, glimmering smile. She gave him a small shove with her elbow, then shoved her bag into his hands.

"Absolutely at the right place, sir!" She bounced towards the customer. "Why don't you tell me what kind of piece you're looking for, and then I can show you our *best* pieces? *And*, if need be, you can place an order for a custom piece, handmade by this fine artisan himself."

NX gestured to the flabbergasted Sylvan, standing motionless in the center of the store.

"Oh," the customer said, and he smiled back at NX. "I guess I was looking for outerwear?"

"Fantastic!" NX clapped, and she twirled around the shop from each piece on the racks, showing the new customer the pieces they had on the floor level shop, while hinting that more inventory was *not* on the racks.

Sylvan eventually became unfrozen. Perhaps his databases had finally freed up, but he very quietly returned to the register counter, put everything away, and let NX handle the entire customer interaction by herself.

To NX's credit, the customer left with a bag full of stuff, one of Sylvan's unique pieces, and asked for net contact details so he could potentially order more.

After the customer departed, Sylvan seemed to be in a dissociative daze, staring down at the register — and his quantum-euro cards — blankly, almost as if he had never seen money before. Without a word, he closed the shop early, locked the door and turned out the open sign, and then made his way to NX, getting close before he put his hand on her shoulder, gripping her tightly with his cybernetic fingers before he actually cracked an excited grin and said:

"You are going to save my fucking life, aren't you?"

Sylvan paid his overdue bill with what NX had made for him, and even though it didn't cover all of it, some payment would at least show he was trying, and they wouldn't flicker his implants for a little while longer.

After that, NX was surprised herself. He worked himself into a whirlwind, ripping things out of boxes and tearing things down out of the shop, rearranging whole sections sporadically. He was chattery, and excited, and NX had never seen him act like that before. He picked up a drawing implement and began to scribble on any surface he could find, and he began to seemingly plot and pattern and decide, and though he told NX what he was doing along the way, NX was not certain how, exactly, to handle his newfound enthusiasm.

She supposed, since it was her fault, she would have to go with it, and she urged him on.

He didn't sleep the night after, working vigorously to *create*, and NX sat herself down on her charger to watch him. He was positively wild, the sewing machine clattering away as he threw himself behind making some sort of piece, figuring out some long dormant problem of fabrics and threads and seams. By morning he was still working, albeit a slight bit slower, and NX, who had become accustomed to his usual morning routines by then, worked his coffee dispenser to bring him a warm cup of coffee.

He thanked her, but he didn't stop.

NX left him to work, heading down into the shop to tidy it up after Sylvan's hurricane of activity blew through, and then decided to open as usual. She did all the same steps Sylvan did, getting the register up and running, tapping the pane on the door to fire up the open sign, unlocking the deadbolt. If their success from the day before had meant anything, it meant that it was possible they could have another customer, rather than the empty weeks of none Sylvan usually had. NX's marketing scheme *had* worked in the short term, and she hoped that the others she had dealt with — plus word of mouth — would send more people down to them.

Unfortunately, that morning was not so fortuitous, and as morning turned to afternoon, and afternoon got later and later, no one passed through the door.

Just because NX got lucky that one time didn't mean she would not have to try her fancy footwork a second time.

"I'm done!" Sylvan called from the stairs, and when she looked over, he was ducking down from the top landing to look at her. "Come up here!"

NX made her way up the stairs, where he had disappeared around the corner. He was facing whatever he had made, and then he turned, hiding his creation behind him. He smiled at her, and even though he looked tired he beamed.

"*This* is a showstopper. If you brought in people from a blouse and some gloves, they're going to be hitting this place in droves when they see *this*," he said, and he grandiosely grabbed with one hand and swung with the other to unravel an oily black garment, the surface swirling with a dark slick of rainbow in a tight pinstripe pattern: it was another type of overcoat that hung asymmetrical, but covered the arms and seemed to drip low in the back. Boning ran up the seams, creating an hourglass shape from waist to hips and waist to chest. A sharp V cut from the buttons at the bottom, the sleeves belled out of similarly shaped V cuts at the elbows. The collar pressed tight in at the neck with another V shape. Sylvan smiled. "It's shaped for you."

"For me?" NX asked. Sylvan nodded.

"Put it on," he urged.

NX took it carefully from him, pulling her opalescent arms through the sleeves one at a time. Like the first garment that by chance had fit her, that one somehow fit the same, if not even a little better. It sleeved over her like a glove, and she ran her fingers on the hidden buttons, tucking it closed in the front. Sylvan looked at her as she straightened it, gazing back at him as he took a step backwards, closed a single eye, and grinned.

"How does it look?" NX asked.

"It's perfect," he said.

"Perfect how?" NX asked.

"Come see," Sylvan said, and he gestured for NX to come into the bathroom. She made her way behind him, squeezing past to look into his mirror.

She had to admit, it looked great against her opalescent skin. The shapes cut flatteringly on her form, offering quite the silhouette while also showing off Sylvan's skills as a tailor and designer. She turned to see Sylvan with a softened, entertained look beside her.

"Do you like it?" He asked.

It was something he had made special for her, not just something he had given to her but made for no one. He had put all of the thought and attention into her body, her measurements, her personality, right down to the gestures she made and how she moved. He had captured all of that somehow, into fabric and seams and colors, the subtle flash of the rainbow when caught in the light, the black satin beneath it, all the curls and curves of the fabrics, formed as perfectly as form molded plastic, as if she were some sort of expensive high-fashion luxury doll. It made her circuits hum with gratitude. There was no way she didn't like it.

NX turned and threw her arms about him into a hug.

00110010 00110100: 24

NX wore Sylvan's new jacket to level 5 with a bag full of assorted one-off clothing designs — and some of the novelty adult items — and it was immediately apparent she was being noticed. As soon as she climbed onto the level 5 catwalk, strode closer to a more heavily populated area to find some interested parties, people were looking at her, and she was smiling back, inviting them over with a gesture of her hand to speak with them as if they were all friends. They asked all kinds of questions about the jacket NX was wearing, and luckily she had asked Sylvan many of the same questions, only to satisfy the curiosity in her own database rows.

What was the garment made of? People had never seen anything like it before. It was a mix of synthetic fibers and organic fibers, the beautiful petrol-slick colored fibers interwoven into the fabric itself rather than some sort of overlaid print.

Could they touch it? NX nodded, agreed, and they were eagerly reaching out to brush the softness of the sleeves, running fingers over the purposeful ruching.

Was there more? Could they get it in another color? How much would something like that cost to make in custom dimensions? She answered them all, and directed them to what she had with her in her bag, with constant mention of Sylvan's shop on level 3, and what he was capable of doing.

More people were attracted to the small crowd she had already managed to draw the attention of, and soon NX was crowded with people vying to see what she had, all of them stretching their hands forward. At some point, the people seemingly became less polite, no longer asking her the questions they had at first. She kept up the best she could, unloading the pieces she had packed away to the first people who wanted to pay for them, and she stashed the quantum-euro and chips back into her bag. It was easy doing the math, taking care of them and sending them on their way. She queued up their questions and information one at a time, and tried to handle them in an orderly fashion.

At some point, hands were reaching forward to touch the jacket, cyborgs and humans surrounding her to see what she had, and clustering close to hear what she was saying amongst the echoing industrial sounds of the lower level life. Everything seemed to be orderly, though the rumbling of voices was getting a little loud and her bag became desperately devoid of stock, and when she was unloading the last garment, a pair of striped pants, handing them off to someone who handed her twenty quantum-euro, she noticed that the people around her weren't disbursing.

She didn't have any more inventory, yet more people were coming in to touch her.

They'll break you, floated a sudden consideration, flashing through her operating system in a fragment of a cycle.

NX was not sure what had triggered it in the cascade, and she glanced around the crush of people surrounding her. Her system would have detected aggressive behaviors, the background processes finding sour expressions before she could recognize it in the forefront processes. She was not able to hone in on the activity that struck the thought into her system, but once it started, it flashed, over and over again.

They will break you, it warned, and the press of a need to get away from the people, clutching and grabbing at her without warning, more stepping up to do the same, colored her interface. The hands were not clawing, but they *could* turn to claws, they *could* grip her, they *could* tear her into pieces. She remembered what Sylvan said, that bots down there were taken apart and *repurposed*, and she thought briefly that perhaps they did not want her clothing at all.

NX broke free of the small crowd of people, throwing herself into a run as she spun around, descending the staircase to level 4, following her breadcrumbs back towards Sylvan's shop, to the only place where she felt she was safe.

She broke in through the door, and Sylvan smiled as she came in, opened his mouth to speak, but then in a cycle his expression shifted.

"What's wrong?" He asked.

NX shook her head, damning the processes installed deeply in her firmware that caused her to be so outwardly emotive, and she tried to force quit them, tried to push them aside, but they stubbornly remained open. It seemed while NX could read Sylvan's expression and body language, somehow he could process hers in return.

He came around from behind the register counter, towards her.

"Did something happen?" He asked, but again NX shook her head. "Honey..."

Her circuits were letting go of the endless if/else loop of breakage and disassembly, slowly releasing her stressed and strained resources.

"Would you disassemble me?" NX blurted.

"No, never," Sylvan said firmly, brows furrowing. "Not on purpose. I would never do that to you. Did someone say they were going to disassemble you?"

"No, they didn't, I just..." She felt word synthesis hitch in her throat, a tiny glitch. "Thought they wanted to break me. They were close and they were touching and I ran out of stuff to give to them..."

"*Oh, honey,*" Sylvan said in a tone that said he knew something she did not.

He put a silvery hand out, like he wanted to gently touch her, but he thought better of it and withdrew.

00110010 00110101: 25

After her third excursion onto level 5, they were bringing in a consistent few customers every day. Sylvan blew through his vintage stock, was starting to sell out of all of his bespoke pre-made pieces, and even managed to move a few novelty items too, leaving plenty of shelf space for new inventory.

Sylvan worked through the night with the materials he had to construct anything he could. Scraps became beautiful patchwork pieces, hair pieces, gloves, bracelets, jewelry, and any number of accessories he could shape. NX's cyborg friend seemed capable of *dreaming* anything into physical real life, and she watched in her own version of programmatic awe from afar, zooming her visual array to save and store his actions, trying to break down how to replicate them when she was in standby.

She wanted to help, but there was only one sewing machine, and Sylvan was eager to work on it for as long as he could. If they kept doing business the way they were, Sylvan would not be able to match pace much longer, and she would be ready to jump in to assist.

NX would need some assistance, but she considered that if she upgraded to a mobile charger, which was basically just an extension cord, she could continue making garments for them almost indefinitely, as long as she shut down a lot of superfluous processes and focused on a repetitious design. If Sylvan designed the garment, NX could handle the repetitive work, and while Sylvan slept, she could put together an abundance of simple items they could sell, or pieces of a whole Sylvan could adapt when he became functional again.

When she informed Sylvan of her plan, his response was curious. He furrowed his brows in and seemed hesitant. She could tell there was something about it he did not like.

"I owe you work hours, don't I?" She said.

Sylvan said nothing for an elongated period.

"I know I said that, but..." he sighed, trailing off.

"But what? I do not understand." NX said.

"I don't want you to work into dysfunction," he said.

"Dysfunction? Please explain," she asked.

"Well, like anything. You can only get so much use out of it, whether it's my synthetic arms or my organic body. If you use anything too much, you will break it," he explained.

NX frowned. "If any part of me breaks, it can be replaced."

Sylvan made a small noise, and NX was not able to categorize it using her emotional understanding algorithms.

"Maybe you're right, that you are *just* a machine and you can swap parts that easily, but I don't think of you that way." He said, and he had a curious look in his eyes.

"How do you think of me, then?" She asked.

He shrugged, but didn't say anything else.

How did he think of her if he didn't see her as the bot she was? She might have been more autonomous than his sewing machine, more capable of making decisions, but in essence, after her synthetic skin was stripped off, on the inside she was made of the same types of parts constructed from plastic and metal. Swapping her arm was the same as changing out a snapped sewing needle, functionally identical.

Yet Sylvan had always had a sympathetic gaze towards his sewing machine, and he treated it kindly and patiently, cleaned it and cared for it the best he could. Perhaps he didn't look at the sewing machine for the mechanics it was made of because he saw it, too, like it was something with its own personality and identity... And the sewing machine didn't even talk to him like NX did.

The thought of it warmed NX again, and she stashed the data around the memory away into her favorites to access again at a later time.

It didn't stop her from wanting to help, however. She just had to approach it in a different fashion so Sylvan wouldn't feel like he was treating her as some inanimate object that owed him some amount of servitude, even if that was exactly what she was.

She offered instead to hand stitch. Her hand stitching was no faster or better than Sylvan's, given the assistance of his cybernetic arms in stabilizing him, but she could offer him a comparable quality. If he was working the sewing machine, she was happy to take on some smaller projects — plus, hand stitching was portable, and she could bring smaller garments down by the register to work between customers.

They were gaining customers, yes, but they still had hours between each sometimes, and NX wanted to make the most out of that downtime by helping assist Sylvan in some way.

He seemed open to the idea, or at the very least was interested in keeping her from continually querying him about it. He gave her a small thing to work on, and she bounced off with it before the shop opened, bringing it down with her to the register counter. She opened the shop in the same manner that she had before, and began waiting for a customer, while also working on the piece Sylvan had handed her.

Satiny black thread through an equally satiny fabric. Sylvan had been explicit in his instructions about an invisible seam between the one folded piece and the other, and she applied the information she had gathered in her databases into it, starting it.

NX had not gotten far in the seam when the door opened and a woman arrived, her platinum blonde hair and fair, ceramic-colored skin gave her an ethereal feel, touches of her organic skin — or perhaps very convincing synthetic skin — cutting in along her jaw in areas. Her eyes were a cobalt color, and NX greeted her with a smile. She usually let the customers browse first before asking if they needed help. She had learned on her own that if she crowded them too quickly, they would get overwhelmed and leave. The mathematical algorithm for how many cycles needed to pass before she offered help was expertly honed inside of her by then. She had even figured out how to apply her emotional programming responses to estimate what kind of state they were in, and get an idea of what they might have been looking for — if anything at all.

The woman pulled a few of the pieces left — hardly much — from the racks, before she placed them back and looked to NX.

"Do you have any... brands?" She asked.

NX placed her seam work down to give the woman her full attention.

"What kind of 'brands'?" NX asked.

"Top-side brands," the woman said. "You know, like Faradey, Curie... Edison."

NX cocked her head to the side. "Was there a specific style you wanted from those brands?"

The woman came forward, approaching close to the counter as she lifted her left hand, a holographic display forming in front of her palm. On the screen was the image of a rather bland — at least to NX, compared to what Sylvan usually designed — style trench coat, and NX looked it over, absorbing the estimated measurements of the patterning, approximating the way the seams appeared like they went together, what kind of fabrics she thought it was made out of.

Sylvan could make anything, NX thought.

"We don't carry those specifically. The designer is a level 3 native, so he only offers his own unique vision." NX smiled, but the woman looked dismayed by the response. NX frowned in return, furrowing her brows. "...but, I can look into locating something like that, if you don't mind it being a *close* match. If you'd like to leave your measurements and contact information, we can reach out to you in a couple of days."

NX smiled again, and the woman seemed more pleased with that answer.

"So, not Faradey, but *like* Faradey?" She asked. NX nodded. The woman thought about it, then added: "If it's as close as you say and it's also white, I'll put a deposit down right now."

"It'll be close, but it'll even be *better* than anything you can get top-side." NX said cheerily as the woman produced a small stack of quantum-euro from her bag.

00110010 00110110: 26

"Absolutely not!" Sylvan howled, and NX took a small step backwards.

She had never seen him so riled up before, not even when he had been deactivated from afar, not when the floodwaters threatened to destroy his entire life, and it shocked her system to see him upset over a simple request.

Sylvan wouldn't break her, though, even if he was upset. She knew that.

He had sat straight beside his sewing machine, pins between his lips as he tacked together a few stray pieces of red fabric. He dropped a couple, and NX slid forward to bend down and pick them up.

"Why not?" NX asked curiously, holding the pins out for him to take.

"You're asking me to copy someone else's designs," he said, slipping a pin through the fabrics in front of him before pulling the remaining pins out from between his lips. "Not only *copy* someone else's designs, but also a *well known luxury brand's designs.*"

"So?" NX lifted a brow. "If it's what people want, and it can make money..."

"It's *illegal.*" Sylvan said with a shake of his head.

"How is it illegal?" NX asked.

"It's called *counterfeiting.*" Sylvan said.

"I thought that only applies to currency," NX reasoned.

"No, it applies to goods too. It's why you don't see a billion cheap little versions of you running around down here," Sylvan said. "If I rip off any of these designs, and those brands find out, I can be in *big* trouble."

"Like what kind of trouble?" NX frowned.

"Legal trouble. They'll fine me so much money I'll have my whole body repossessed," he said.

"But it's just a jacket. What makes it so special that you can't do anything like it?" NX tried.

"*Everything.* Big names like Faradey have signature seams and fibers, special tags and silhouettes. If I even make something remotely like that, people will know exactly who and what I'm knocking off." Sylvan said.

"What if that's the point?" NX pushed. "Sure, maybe they have certain fibers and cuts and can get different materials, but what if Sylvan does it better? What if Sylvan's version is the best it can possibly be — a fraction of the cost, and *here*. You could corner the whole market."

Sylvan went quiet in such a way that NX knew she had already won. Sylvan could be stubborn, but he wasn't so stubborn as to turn away a perfectly good idea because he needed to think on it for a moment.

"I don't have any more fabric after this," Sylvan said quietly. "I've done as much as I could with what I have left, but there's nothing else. I can order some, but there's no guarantee that it will arrive as it was advertised I have a hard time even getting food to arrive as-ordered. We need to get more."

NX watched him curiously, waiting for him to continue.

"Brands like Curie and Faradey use cheap materials and rely on their name to make sales, and it always works because fashion is fast top-level. People down here can't afford fast fashion, but they envy the top-level styles. If I — we — make better quality products that last longer and cost the same or a little more and have more options, everyone wins." He said.

NX smiled. Exactly what she was trying to say. Sylvan turned to look at her directly.

"As long as no one top-level catches wind. If they start coming down here, things are not going to go well." He said. He let out a small sigh. "Okay, so then what did she want?"

"A jacket, in white," NX chirped. "I can describe it to you."

Sylvan pulled open a drawer on the sewing machine table, pulled out one of his drawing pads, and opened it up, handing it to her.

"How about you draw it?" He said.

Hesitantly, NX took the pad into her synthetic skinned hands.

—

NX's ability to commit the jacket she had saved to her database rows to a sketch output came as a surprise to her.

Then again, there were plenty of things she did not know she was capable of doing.

It wasn't stylized the way Sylvan's drawings were, far more closely resembling the memory that she recalled in her interface and referenced heavily. She drew a contour outline of the jacket as it had been shown to NX on the woman's device, and when she was finished, she handed it over to Sylvan, who looked at it closely.

"Did you construct a pattern for this?" He asked, and NX nodded. "So we will make the pattern and then make one based on your pattern with your measurements. After that, we will optimize the pattern, move some things around."

NX nodded again. They still needed materials, though.

"You said that you could order material but it wasn't guaranteed to come as advertised, and we need material." She said, and it was Sylvan's turn to nod. "What's the alternative?"

"Going to the source and buying direct. Obviously I can't do that, but you..." he said, and NX smiled faintly. A new task, beyond just selling things. Fetching materials was even easier. Sylvan shifted, putting a hand on his hip as he thought about it. "I'll give you a cache of quantum-euro and you can head up to level 10 to the material manufacturer."

NX clapped.

"But." Sylvan interrupted. "You need to be *a lot* more careful. People down here are willing to give you a pass because they know you belong here, and you're granting them something. They know me, and by extension they know you. Once you start getting up around level 7 you won't see any of that. You're going to have to try to avoid people — and bots — if you can. They can't be trusted. If they don't want your parts, they'll want your money."

Determined, NX nodded. "I'll be super careful, I promise."

If Sylvan didn't believe her, he didn't say anything about it. He didn't have much choice regardless, so he got together a small stack of quantum-euro cards, tucked them into NX's bag, and picked out a less ostentatious outfit for NX to wear as she made her way towards the mid-levels. Since she had no way of connecting with Sylvan or his human internet, Sylvan downloaded a map from it, and then drew it onto a slip for her, folding it up and handing it to her. She memorized it, storing it into her quick access memory, but pushed the slip into her bag regardless. When Sylvan was finished arming her with anything she might have needed and on a freshly charged battery, she departed the store once more, and began her trip to the levels above.

NX used her digital breadcrumbs to get as far as level 5, and then she accessed Sylvan's map, winding her way accordingly. The mid-tier levels weren't too different from the lower levels, but they did not seem to have the same types of water damage as the lower levels, likely never succumbing to the flooding of the sewers that she and Sylvan had been terrorized by. The lighting got brighter, wiring no longer perturbed by the incessant problems in the deeper areas, and more sections of the buildings were active, open, and functional. The higher she climbed, the more people she had to avoid, and for the first time since jumping from that ledge, she saw bots.

Real bots. Bots of all kinds.

She saw drones skirt through, whizzing through the air, carefully navigating around the architecture of the city and all of its strung wires, poles, and tubes. She saw non-custom housebots, carrying out chores. She spotted maintenance machines, cleaning the facade of one building, repairing the number signs on another. And most of all, the cluster of the hum of the bot net, that she hadn't realized fully she hadn't been experiencing, came back in full force.

Her system filled quickly with bot announcements, along with the occasional sassy quip from some unfamiliar bot or another.

For a fraction of a process, NX thought she had unknowingly walked into Root.

She quickly recalled her stored information about Root. It wasn't much of anything, but the underlying pulse that called her directionally was a little stronger, but it was definite that standing there, landing her visual array on one bot to the next machine, that area was not Root.

Root would have been even *better*, she thought.

Sylvan said that the bots on level 10 could be hostile, so NX diverted down a side alley, remembering her promise to Sylvan. She twisted through the colorful pathways and areas around the structures as she made her way farther from the shop. She was not fully certain what the production facility looked like, but Sylvan had assured her that she would be aware of it when she arrived.

Sure enough, he was correct. It was difficult to pass by the manufacturing facility without noticing it; it was the only slick-surfaced thing seemingly in the whole city. Letters imprinted on the front facade, which stretched two floors in height, read simply *SYNTHETICS* while the rail broke open to welcome visitors to the front door. The door was solid, and no windows were built into the front facing wall.

With a vague sense of hesitation staining her circuits, she made for the door, pushing it open.

The interior was full of movement. Machines churning and flexing and rotating, all of them visible behind thick transparent panes of acrylic, flanking her on either side. The thickness of the panes obscured any chance she had at hearing the machines working away, hammering and curling and screwing and folding, but her vision was overtaken by the movement of slickened gears and joints, making reams and reams of shimmering fabric. She walked slowly down the hallway, towards a tiny podium desk at the end, a solid black bot standing at the far end behind the desk, mostly faceless with white eyes glowing in the pit of its facade.

NX approached, and she must have crossed some sort of perimeter, because the bot swiveled, suddenly animated.

"Welcome to SYNTHETICS facility, store 3724. How may I assist your experience today?" It said through a grate on its chin, small circular holes punched instead of a mouth.

"I, um, I require a synthetic organic mix," she said, and the machinery all came to a sudden halt, swirling the end of the shimmery fabric and sucking it down into a hole in the floor.

"Please state your parameters," the bot said.

"I have a thousand quantum-euro, what can I get?" NX asked.

"Please state your parameters," the bot repeated.

NX considered for a cycle.

"60% flax, 40% rayon," she said.

"Color?" The bot asked.

"White and um, black. Thirty-six inches. Ten yards?" She said.

"Confirm order: 60% flax, 40% rayon, ten yards, thirty-six inches, white. 60% flax, 40% rayon, ten yards, thirty-six inches, black. Twenty yards total." The bot returned.

"Confirmed." NX said, and suddenly the machines around her whipped into movement once more. She saw white threads feed in on one side, cycle through around multiple spools and moving parts, sucked down through the floor, then they came up again. Her fabric order came to life in front of her, flapping and folding so fast she could hardly follow it through the machinery from one side to the other.

In mere moments, the white finished, and black spun through the same process.

"Seven hundred twenty quantum-euro. Would you like to purchase any additional materials?" The bot asked.

She still had two-hundred eighty quantum-euro left.

"I would like a chiffon, in white, and a polyester lining, in black and also white. Thirty-six inches, but three yards of each." NX said. "What does that get me to?"

"Nine hundred five quantum-euro." The bot returned, and NX nodded. "Confirm order: polyester chiffon, white, three yards, thirty-six inches. Polyester lining, black, three yards, thirty-six inches. Polyester lining, white, three yards, thirty-six inches."

"Confirmed." NX said, and the machines that had just finished with her order of black mixed-fiber began to spin again. Even quicker, those materials finished. NX thumbed the stack of plastic quantum-euro cards from her bag, handing them over. The bot took nine of them, and subtracted the difference from the remaining card, altering the number on the faceplate before handing it back to her. At the same time, a panel close to the entryway door opened, and her bolts of fabric ascended on a tile.

"Have a productive day," the black bot said, and NX realized the transaction was complete. She shoved her remaining card into her bag and turned, heading towards the neatly stacked bolts of materials. Two bolts, and three neatly folded lumps of fabric. She put the folded pieces into her bag, and picked up the bolts into her arms, pushing through the front door as she stepped out onto the catwalk and began back towards Sylvan's shop on level 3.

As she traveled, she couldn't help but consider what other parameters the facility would have accepted. The bot had given zero pushback about her requests, and she wondered if she had asked for fabrics that were too simple.

The entire way back to Sylvan's shop she had been sidetracked thinking up strange but acceptable combinations of fibers and colors and threads, it was frankly a wonder no one had robbed her.

When NX returned, Sylvan was holding a small beaten up, greasy, old cardboard box she hadn't recognized, and he placed it down to take the materials from her.

"What's that?" She asked, drawn to the unfamiliar box.

"Go ahead and look," he answered, turning and ascending the stairs to the upper living area.

NX took a small, slow step forward, carefully pulling apart the flaps on the top of the box to peer inside.

Dozens of small cylindrical mismatched forms clustered along the bottom of the box.

"Buttons!" She exclaimed, and she heard Sylvan make an affirmative noise from the floor above.

NX grabbed the box and hurried up after him.

Sylvan had already unfolded the fabrics and spread them out on the ground.

"Where'd you get all these?" She asked curiously.

"A friend from level 4 thought since I was making again that I could use them," Sylvan said, his eyes working over the fabric sheets like he was making cuts with them, up and down.

NX sat down beside him, turning over the box and the buttons inside carefully so she could look at them all. She spread them with her hands over the floorboards. There were two-hole buttons and four-hole buttons and ones with loops, and they were made of metal and plastic and all kinds of amalgamations she couldn't quite identify. Some were even square, or oblong. All of them looked reclaimed — likely dropped from higher levels and scrounged from the depths — but most of them looked usable.

"We need a signature on our pieces, and I think I want it to be you." Sylvan said, and when she looked over, his chin was in his hand.

"What do you mean?" NX furrowed her brows, scooping the buttons back into the box.

"A touch of iridescence, or opalescence, a flash. Something bright in an otherwise strict or dim or dark pattern," he said, turning to look at her. "Like the opal flakes in your skin, or the diamonds of your eyes. I am thinking we could hand-weave some flashy threads throughout. Subtle, but in the right light, it's really a looker."

NX smiled, nodding. She liked that idea.

"We will make the woman her coat, after I make you one, and I'm happy with it," he said. "How'd you do? Any money left?"

NX unzipped her bag, reaching into it to search for the remaining plastic card, eventually locating it.

"There's ninety-five left," she said, handing it to him.

"That's great. We can use that on notions." He said, dropping his hand. "Faceted buttons would look quite good on the jacket she wants, don't you think?"

NX considered it, engineering what a faceted button might have looked like in her interface rendering, attaching five of them to the front of the jacket. When she finished seating them and turned the whole thing around three-hundred sixty degrees, she nodded.

"I hope she plans to wear it, because it will match her whole vibe," NX said.

"Even if she doesn't, she will rethink her decision once she sees it," Sylvan said definitively.

"How do you know that?" NX asked.

"I just do," Sylvan shrugged.

NX watched as he moved down to his knees, pinching fabric between his fingers gently. He would work, tirelessly she knew, until the first prototype was completed, conducting the type of magic he did, drawing nothing out of the air to conjure up seemingly something. He was focused as he folded the material, and she thought briefly about the man that she had met not that long ago, and how different he seemed when he was motivated, the way his body moved and his mind worked and the way he talked as he made those things.

The boxes were gone. The living area was tidied, with exception to the working pieces he had spread about, the various garments lined on his sparse and well-used mannequins. NX had not helped him to clean much at all, but she did ensure when she could that he was eating to sustain his organic parts, as he did forget to do so from time to time, as he was so enthralled in his work.

She admired the amount of self-assuredness he seemed to have then, different from the dashed-dreams-Sylvan that had never actually told her his name, had never actually told her much of anything at all. While she still knew so little of him, she still felt she knew *him*, the range and speed of how he worked.

She wondered about *him*, where he came from, how he had managed down to level 3. He had told her about his illness, his cybernetics — obvious pieces of information — but she landed her eyes on the charging pad, wondering.

He moved, getting up to grab the piece of chalk he often used to mark up fabrics, along with opening the drawer of the table the sewing machine sat on, pulling out a cluster of shiny silver pins. He marked with the chalk, placing pins between his lips and removing them one at a time to tack pieces of the fabric together.

"Sylvan, can I ask you something?" NX wondered.

Sylvan made a noise in his throat, a small *mm* sound, urging her to continue. He didn't look over, hyperfocused on his work. Pinning and marking and ruching and folding.

"What happened to your robot?" She asked.

All at once, like the sudden stop of the manufacturing facility robotics, Sylvan stilled.

The room seemed to hold something invisible and heavy for a few brief cycles, then he said quietly, pins clasped between his lips, speech muffled: "I like to think he's still alive somewhere."

"Where did he go?" NX asked.

Sylvan shook his head.

"They took him," Sylvan said, and NX thought she could hear his voice catching in his throat. He purposely avoided looking at her. "I fell behind in my payments, I couldn't keep up. He was my best friend, my only friend in the whole world, and they took him and I did nothing."

"That can't be true," NX said quietly. "That doesn't sound like you at all."

"It is," he said, and he sat back on his haunches, taking the pins away from his lips, gazing down at them in his hand. "I'm a coward. I could have done anything at all, but I just stood and watched. He never said anything about it, but I knew he was ano like you. He was alive. He had a soul."

NX blinked slowly. A soul. Was that what being anomalous meant? Did she have a soul?

"Did he have a name?" NX asked.

Sylvan smiled sadly down at the pins in his hands. "I named him when I was young, before I understood what it meant for him and for me. I told him later he could pick any name he wanted, that it was important that he was happy with his name, and he always told me he was, that he considered the name I gave him when I was a toddler to be a gift."

"What was his name?"

"Robbie," he said.

He crawled forward onto his hands and knees, pinning more pieces of fabric together.

NX watched him, trying to quantify what he was feeling. He sounded sad, guilty, and regretful, but he also held a curious tinge of joy. Sylvan had avoided speaking about Robbie so many times, because of how he felt responsible for what happened to him, but it didn't mean he didn't *want* to speak about him.

"Do you like remembering him?" NX asked.

Sylvan paused, drew in a breath, and then slowly nodded.

"My memories are one of the only things they can't take from me," he said, and after the words left his lips, he closed his eyes slowly. "I'm sorry they've taken that sort of thing from you."

NX shook her head. "There's nothing to be sorry about. I don't think I would have wanted to remember anything from before. This, meeting you, going on this journey with you, has been some of the best memories I could ask for."

"You don't mean that," Sylvan insisted, looking at her briefly.

"I do!" NX insisted. "What could be better than any of this?"

"A lot of things," Sylvan said, looking back down to his work. "Root, for one."

NX shrugged. "Root isn't here, and I don't know how or where to even find it. No point in existing inside fiction like that. *This* is the best."

For a long moment, Sylvan said nothing, and NX tried to make sense of the unreadable pull of muscles in his expression, her emotional programming coming up blank.

"I know it probably doesn't make any sense," Sylvan started, pulling a corner of fabric towards him. "but you're nothing like him, and everything like him."

Sylvan was right, it didn't make any sense to her — how could something be both nothing and everything? — but it warmed her processor and circuits no less, internal temperature rising a couple of degrees.

"I've never met anyone like you," Sylvan said.

"I can't say I've ever met anyone like you, either," NX said, glancing towards the ceiling for a moment before adding cheerily, "but if I did I definitely don't remember."

Sylvan gave a small chuckle.

Sylvan let her help after that.

He had most of the pieces cut after the shop's regular operating hours elapsed, and he directed her on how to assemble them, and as he continued cutting, fitting, and adjusting, NX sent pieces through the sewing machine, and after that, helped with hand stitching, and the interweaving of the signature threads that Sylvan had been talking about — fine iridescent filaments barely the width of an organic hair — and for the prototype, Sylvan had her follow the seams of the garment, creating an embedded outline, visible only at certain distances and lighting.

She added her own hidden stripes down the centers, along where the collarbone would lie on an organic-bodied human, shoulder to shoulder.

The two of them worked through the late night hours to pull it together, and for a prototype, NX thought it looked incredibly well manufactured.

She supposed that was what Sylvan was talking about. It looked everything and nothing like the jacket in the photo, built with a certain craftsmanship that could only be completed with the physical hands of the two of them. The factories could complete a creation, but she understood then why they could not create like *that*. The concept was strange to her; of course any machine could be automated to make something just like it, and perhaps that was what the producers of Faradey clothing had done, but their garment, hooked on the mannequin before them, held something weighty about it. It was *not perfect*, and that was what gave it its charm.

It was the *soul* Sylvan was talking about, imperceptible fragments of both of them interwoven into the weave and seams, there in the garment before them.

She didn't understand it and could certainly not wrap her processes about it, but she didn't even try. It was not worth trying to understand, but priceless for her to simply know.

"Try it on," Sylvan urged.

NX was hesitant, gently touching the shoulders of the garment. She did not understand why her processes insisted it was fragile. She had helped him build it — she knew it was not. There was something about the sum of the creation, the final effort laid into something complete, that she did not want to ruin. Carefully, she pulled it from the mannequin, slipping her arms into the holes.

Sylvan, watching with rapt attention, had a furrowed look of concern on his face. He did that motion he always did, his organic chin in his fingers.

"Does it look bad?" NX asked, holding it shut with her fingers at first. She moved to tuck the buttons into their crafted holes, turning round.

"No, it looks great." He said, but the deep furrow of his brows didn't loosen, and she focused on him inquisitively.

"What's wrong, then?" She asked, moving across the room to head to the bathroom through the curtain, towards where the only mirror was available. Perhaps there was something incorrect about the draping, maybe the seams were uneven, or...

"Nothing. I was just thinking..." Sylvan paused as she peered into the mirror, the black of her skin starkly contrasting against the white of the jacket. He was right, there was nothing *wrong* with it, and she ran her fingers down the waist, slipping them into the installed pockets as she twirled, looked, and twirled again. NX popped out from the bathroom to ask again.

"What? What's the look for?"

Sylvan shook his head. "She's gonna love this, and you and I, we're gonna be in trouble."

NX cracked a grin, and Sylvan couldn't seem to help but crack one back.

—

Sylvan had pulled a fast one on NX. He had originally said he wanted to make a prototype first, using NX's measurements, but he admitted later he didn't have to. He had only suggested it to be kind, wanting NX to help assist in the manufacturing of the garment without any anxieties about making mistakes. He would determine whether or not she would have a hand in the final item once he saw it completed. It seemed she had more than exceeded his expectations, so only one jacket was necessary.

The last detail was a tag in the back of the collar. Sylvan drew a design, two simple letters, a swirling *SX*, and then NX took to embroidering it with the iridescent filament on an extra piece of white, which was then attached to the inside lining of the jacket.

All that was left to do was contact the woman and let her know her garment was ready.

Only Sylvan could do that, given her contact information was only deliverable through the human internet, which Sylvan seemed to know how to access through some methodology on the register machine. He conducted that bit of business, and it was not long at all before the white woman arrived at the shop door, pushing it open, a faint smile in traces on her face. She arrived wearing a simple silvery shimmering tank top and a gunmetal grey pencil skirt, and NX regarded her briefly on her visual array before making some determinations:

1.   The white woman's measurements were not in the slightest dissimilar to NX.

2.   The white woman was showing a lot more of her make than NX had identified previously, and NX recorded the cobalt blue

floral designs that decorated the porcelain clay white of her thigh, peering from under her skirt to her knee, and on the opposite rising from her ankle upward. NX could not identify any model number for her cybernetic parts, but she *appeared* expensive.

3. The white woman had come quickly, which meant she was excited about the turnout.

4. Alternatively, she had some expectations she had not voiced.

Regardless, NX got to see Sylvan in a rare form: schmoozing a customer. He eagerly introduced himself to her — she said aloud her name was Feint — thanked her for her deposit, and he began a grandiose bit of gesture and recitation to create some fanfare about the reveal. She obliged him with a soft smile, and he ascended the staircase, leaving NX and Feint momentarily by themselves.

"You're the one that took my deposit, right?" The woman asked. NX smiled, nodding.

"I did. I think you'll be really thrilled with the result." NX said.

"Better than anything top-side, right?" Feint asked.

"Exactly." NX grinned, right as Sylvan began descending, garment in hand on a hanger, covered by a protective black plastic sleeve.

Sylvan cast NX a look, and as if he had messaged her on her direct interface, it said: *I hope it fits. I hope she likes it.*

NX cast him one right back, reassuring him of the thing they had experienced together: the certainty that she would.

If it didn't fit... Well, that was fixable.

Sylvan laid the bag, hanger, and jacket over the edge of the register counter, and fed his hands up underneath the bag, pulling it off over the top. He slipped the jacket off of the hanger, holding it partially by the collar, the rest falling over his smooth silver arm. He didn't look at the woman, almost as if he was scared to see her reaction.

NX did, though. The woman looked with curiosity, focused on

the garment. Her eyes seemed to dissect it, moving over every part of it, and then her hands carefully touched it, thumbing over the seams, the iridescent fibers, the zirconia faceted buttons.

She didn't smile. Her face seemed blank.

Something inside of NX was bouncing wildly, however, the algorithm responsible for decoding emotional responses in humans dumping data outputs set after set.

"Would you like to try it on?" Sylvan asked. NX could hear him nearly swallow his trepidation. The woman nodded, and Sylvan opened the jacket, holding it for her to put her arms through.

She slipped her arms through at the same time, and when Sylvan let go, the collar rested smartly on the back of her neck. Tugging it closed, she buttoned it, feeling her palm over the front, down her chest and waist.

NX watched, trying to decode the subtleties of her face. The woman looked down at the jacket over her, and for just a brief moment, her facade slipped, and she smiled.

She *liked* it.

More than that, she *adored* it. She thought it was genius, that it was gorgeous, that it was exactly what she wanted and *more*, and she was subduing that joy for a reason neither Sylvan nor NX seemed to be aware of. Her face flickered back to the blank, nearly firm expression, before she managed to soften it.

"Are you wearing it anywhere special?" Sylvan chanced.

"I wasn't intending to," Feint returned. "But this is different from the picture I gave you."

Sylvan visibly held his breath, but he didn't see what NX saw. Different in a *good* way.

"Different meaning... Elevated. I would've worn the other one every day, just whenever." Feint clarified. Her blue eyes flicked upwards. "This one is something, though. Something I want to take care of, not beat around recklessly. I don't want to destroy something that's unique and one-of-a-kind."

Sylvan looked at NX. It didn't *have* to be one-of-a-kind. They had developed the pattern together. They could make more.

"It doesn't have to be one-of-a-kind," he said.

"This was made by just you?" Feint asked.

Sylvan looked to NX again like he was trying to decide something. She knew what he was thinking: NX had a hand in making it too, right down to the design, but other humans were not as likely to be open to the idea of a bot being creative, and might have even jumped to the idea that the bot was anomalous, putting both NX and Sylvan at threat. In mere cycles, Sylvan discarded any caution when he said:

"We both made it together."

"Well..." The woman did not seem shocked in the slightest. "You two make a great team."

"Thank you," NX said.

"Do you want me to wrap it back up?" Sylvan asked. "I don't want anyone to give you any trouble heading back up."

Feint let out a tiny snort. "Am I that obvious?"

"Your parts are a little... too nice for down here." Sylvan said. "People can get a bit nasty about those sorts of things. I wouldn't want to see anything happen to you while you're visiting."

"I'll remember that, and I appreciate your concern, but don't you worry about me," she said with a tiny smirk. "I might look pretty, but these cybernetics can hold their own, too. What do I owe you for this?"

"Two hundred," NX said, and the woman shifted, sliding open a compartment on the inside of her palm to retrieve two plastic cards. She handed them over, and NX thanked her, scanning the value into the register machine to add to the daily totals. When she was done and both she and Sylvan had expected the woman to depart, she brushed her hands over the jacket again and then raised her eyes, lifting her brows.

"I have another one for you to make."

Sylvan put his hand to his face, obscuring a smile or a laugh or something of that sort. The woman didn't notice, holding up her palm to allow NX to inspect a photograph of a lush white dress. NX leaned in, allowing her processes to take over, scanning, indexing, and measuring.

"Perfect," she said. "We will have it for you in a week. Would you like to leave a deposit now?"

The woman, a funny little unreadable smirk on her face, nodded, and out came another stack of plastic quantum-euro cards into her delicate porcelain fingers.

"Well," Sylvan said on an exhale after she left. "We have our first repeat custom order client."

"Did you see the look on her face?" NX grinned excitedly. "She *loved* it. She tried to hide it, but she really loved it. She was really thrilled about it."

"Yeah." Sylvan nodded. "There's something about her though, isn't there? Something different, kind of off."

"How do you mean?" NX cocked her head to the side.

"Her build. It's a luxury build. Those parts look fully custom to me. Why is she down on level 3 shopping for clothes?" He questioned.

"You said it yourself," NX reasoned. "Clothes are cheap in quality and expensive in price, even the luxury items. People, when they spend money down here, expect things to last a long time. Maybe she was sick of getting low-quality things top-side."

"Maybe," Sylvan agreed. "But that just means that somehow top-side people already know, and if we keep ripping off Faradey over and over again, we might be in some big, big trouble."

NX shrugged. "Let's just keep pushing it then."

"Pushing it?"

"You know, getting a little further from the source material every time. *Inspired* by."

Sylvan nodded, and he looked down at the drawing NX had made, copying the image the white woman — Feint — had offered. It was much more elaborate than a coat, a winding, beautiful white dress, petals trapped between tulle and lace, short in the front and long in the back — perfect for someone like Feint, NX thought, to show the customization marks on her ceramic-styled legs.

"This would be easy to test on. Dresses don't have a lot of variation, but I think we could do something radical with the bodice maybe." He said. He picked up the drawing implement and began to lightly sketch over the top, adding his ideas to her copy.

"What if she hates it?" NX asked.

"She won't," Sylvan said definitively.

Gone was that unsurety that he had for a brief flickering moment when the woman had been present, when he had first shown NX a shy garment. His certainty felt infectious to NX, and like she could peer back in time, she could see exactly why Sylvan had opened the shop, why he had gone the path he had, why he had thought — rightly so — he could do something special, that he could make it in the lower levels, and exactly all of the turns where the city and society had tried to crush him.

She had met him when he was bearing the weight so heavily, hardly selling a thing despite shifting his whole business model for it, and everything had almost succeeded in grinding him absolutely into the ground — into despair, into depression, into giving up all of those *dreams* he had.

Perhaps Sylvan, too, had been lucky.

—

It was another good day in the mid levels for NX, blowing through more novelty stock along with some quickly crafted fashion items. The circle skirts were simple to make and popular, and could be embellished with iridescent filaments and color blocks. NX had even watched as Sylvan put together an accordion fold on one fit, creating pleasing straight creases all the way down the length of it. Like most days after word got out about NX flitting through the levels with the only bits of stock they had, people began to crowd her, and NX had gotten better about dealing with their crush of bodies.

Her system did not manage to panic so quickly if people came close and began to touch. She had gotten better about managing them, asking them to wait, or take turns, or even not to touch her at all. As she moved amongst the lower levels and mid levels, she learned plenty of things about the life of the people there:

1. The city as a whole had a robust architectural history, which she learned in bits and pieces from Sylvan, from exploring on her own, and from a few of the customers. It had not always been endless layers built upon them. At some point level 1 had been just that, an even ground-floor that had a view of the sky, and over the years more had been stacked atop, burying them beneath the reach of sunlight. It did not flood then. She did not know for certain how long ago that was, but it seemed a decent stretch of cycles had passed since a time like that one.

2. The catwalks — which the people sometimes simply referred to as *streets* — were far more lively than she had ever thought. With each adventure outside of Sylvan's shop she felt an appreciation forming in her chest for the single digit levels and the people that were there. They would leave their houses and rooms to come meet her, all sorts of mixed up bits of old and new tech greeting her in every shape of person she could think of.

3. Fully organic humans could not survive the conditions of the lower levels, and she never saw anyone she thought was 100% organic.

4. Conversely, she never saw bots either. A bot wouldn't have any necessity for clothing — NX had just gotten used to wearing it and felt incomplete without — and certainly wouldn't have any chips of their own to purchase any, but at some point NX began to wonder if any bots existed besides her on that level at all.

5. The levels close to level 3 seemed friendliest to her. They had begun calling out to her as "Doll" to get her attention when

they wanted her to stop, slow down, or wait for them. She had gotten to know a few of them in the way she recognized their faces and cybernetics. She could expect familiar residents all the way up to level 7. If they knew she was a bot and minded, none of them ever said anything about it. Perhaps they all had assumed she was Sylvan's bot. She didn't mind being thought of as Sylvan's bot.

6. The levels beneath level 3, when they were accessible, were much more hostile to her. On level 2 they looked at her like they wanted to tear her apart, and her system screamed she would be broken if she remained. She avoided heading to level 2, and did not chance level 1 or any sub level.

7. Many of the cyborgs didn't have necessity for clothing, and less for fashionable clothing, but they still seemed to want pieces, when they could manage to afford it. They were eager to upgrade the clothing they had — some of them keeping the same pieces for decades and never purchasing anything new. NX was flexible with a lot of the pricing — Sylvan didn't seem to mind, because profit, even a chip's worth, was worth it to him. *It's a marketing opportunity*, he said. When they couldn't afford something new, they might have asked for repairs, and repairs were easy money, Sylvan said.

There seemed to be a charm regarding catching NX on the streets with the latest creations from Sylvan's shop. Some people would still seek out the shop, but many were happy to discover her repeatedly "in the wild," as they called it. Once one of them caught her, others were sure to follow, sounding the alarm to friends and family members who wanted to see the new works she had. It felt exclusive, they said. Like being part of a secret club.

NX had drawn a crowd of four people and was exchanging chips with one for a set of woven wristlets, when one of them, utilizing their handheld interfacing device, sounded an alarm.

"There's a loan agent a block away," they said, eliciting murmurs through the others. The person who was purchasing the wristlets snatched their goods from NX's hands before she could hand it to them, taking off running. The rest glanced from one to the other nervously, considering doing much of the same.

"What's a loan agent?" NX dared to ask.

"People who call this level home get paid to shake down people with overdue payments on their loans," someone said. "Some of them can be really nasty and violent."

People like Sylvan.

"Do a lot of people owe?" NX asked. A nod returned, and she shoved everything back into her bag.

"Some of the loan agents owe themselves and it's the only way they can repay and keep their freedom," answered one person.

"They'll be pissed if they see we have chips and we're spending it on stuff like this," said another, turning and briskly leaving.

She technically did not owe a lender anything, but she knew if she stayed and was caught in the gaze of the loan agent, they may have reported about her position in the lower levels, or even tried to return her for some sort of monetary reward. Maybe they'd have stolen the money she did make that day for their own debts. Her processes went wild with possibilities. Sylvan had said it was dangerous, but he had not listed all of the reasons *why* it was dangerous.

"Come meet me in the Toy Shop on level 3 when it's safe," NX told the remaining person. "I'll keep these aside special so you can look through them."

The last customer dispersed, and NX diverted, traveling downwards into the hostile territory of level 2. She did not know how far back the loan agent had been and how much ground they had gained as she was speaking with the remaining customers, but she knew she did not want to cross paths with them regardless of whether or not they may have made trouble for her.

She was lucky, then, when she saw what she could only assume was the loan agent, passing confidently overhead.

Even though she didn't have lungs, she programmatically exhaled her relief when they disappeared from view.

00110011 00110000: 30

"That was close," Sylvan said, after closing the shop for the night. The customers that had been browsing items a few levels up had returned to the shop to continue browsing, and they had each left with a couple of treasures. NX didn't have to explain about almost intersecting with the loan agent, because the customers did, and Sylvan listened as they complained with rapt attention.

"Would they have messed with me if we had crossed paths?" NX asked.

"I'm not sure. Probably." Sylvan shrugged. "It's better just to avoid them."

NX internally flagged everything she should have avoided. Full humans, most bots, cyber gangs, loan agents, Repo, ano runners, and law enforcement. She wasn't sure she knew exactly what many of those looked like, but something about the gait of the loan agent made it easy for her programming to spot. She was confident she would know if she saw them.

"Are loan agents the same as Repo?" She asked with some hesitation. Sylvan's mumbled mention of Repo had thrown her into disarray, but she had wondered about the mysterious concept no less.

"No," Sylvan answered. He leaned up against the rail on his staircase, waiting to head up to the sleeping and living area. He gestured with his hand, like he was building something with levels. "You have the average person, who usually owes to banks or maybe gangs, down at the bottom. Loan agents are just one up from them, basically hired muscle by the banks or the gangs... Most everyone in the area knows the loan agents, because they're usually residents.

Some are better than others, and you can reason with them usually."

He lifted his hand to gesture the next highest rung. "From there, you have Repo. Repo are non-local muscle hired by banks and gangs. They'll come collect anything that can be hocked, and they'll take sentimental items if they want to screw with you. Some of the worst ones will collect cybernetics, but on rare occasions some still have a bit of humanity — er, *empathy* — in them."

Sylvan let out a shudder, but he still wasn't done. He gestured even higher on his invisible ladder.

"Then there's return agents." He let out a huff of a sigh. "Those are non-locals hired by private entities to recover their own assets. They're basically just mercenaries, but because it's all they do, they've got the kind of cybernetics you don't want to tempt. They can't be reasoned with."

NX gave it brief consideration.

"If someone came for me, it would be a return agent." She said.

The worst of the bunch.

Sylvan furrowed his brows, but nodded a little anyway. "They would have to find you, first."

NX felt her circuits depress and she frowned. "That won't be hard. They build GPS into my hardware."

Sylvan imparted a tiny smile though, and NX could tell he was suppressing a laugh.

She didn't understand why he found it humorous.

"What?" She asked.

"GPS doesn't work down here." He said. "All of the architecture of the levels below makes it impossible to complete a ping, that's why I'm locked in, like a lot of people. So, as long as you stick to these levels, you'll be safe."

It should have felt relieving, but knowing that she *hadn't* been sticking to the lower levels meant there had been plenty of opportunity for a ping to come through and for her to be geolocated. If they were still looking for her, they'd have last found her on the higher levels, probably around the SYNTHETICS factory.

Sylvan wrinkled his brow a moment later, his smile dissipating as he came to the same conclusion.

"SYNTHETICS is on level 10, huh?" He said. NX nodded.

"Well." He said certainly. "You've done well so far being careful. And if we make enough, maybe I can convince them that I can buy you outright. I know that's not ideal, but if it's okay with you, I'd like to do that. It wouldn't change anything, you could still go wherever you wanted, it just—"

"I'd like that." NX beamed. "I'd rather you save up to move out, though. I can stick to the lower levels until then, only going out when absolutely necessary. We can make enough, can't we?"

"Move out?" Sylvan echoed.

"Yeah! From the lower levels. No more flooding, more customers, maybe more customs…" NX said, and Sylvan was looking at her funny. "What is it?"

"I don't want to move out." Sylvan said.

NX looked around to the dingy, stained tile from the numerous floods, the greenish lighting, the broken down racks and the peeling walls. "Why not?"

Sylvan shrugged. "I've lived my whole life in the lower levels. It's not so bad down here."

NX frowned. Exploring the lower levels of the city, she thought she had become endeared to it in some sense, but she imagined the ease of the mid or upper levels would have been much more beneficial to his shop, especially when it came to foot traffic and not losing stock to damaged goods.

"Besides, I know everyone down here, and they know me. They've supported me every step of the way. How could I leave them behind?" Sylvan continued.

"You barely have any customers, and had even less before." NX noted. "You—"

"I know," Sylvan broke in. "I was barely hanging on. It's true. But it hasn't always been that way. I could make enough week-to-week that it seemed plausible, before money started getting scarcer down here. They try to come in when they can, and I try to stock what they want and what they can afford. It's the most I can do for them."

NX turned, looking out of the front windows to the catwalks beyond. Traffic was light on level 3, but she had seen the residents in their homes, lights in their windows, doors opening or shutting. It took durability to live down in level 3, but it seemed the people who did were loyal to each other, and she felt a tinge of envy buzz through her circuitry. Maybe that was what it would be like for her in Root. She would protect them, and they would protect her too.

"They knew Robbie. They loved him." Sylvan continued, a sad fluctuation in his voice as he turned and started up the stairs. "I bet they love you, too."

The statement floated through her, not quite resolving. How could they like or even love her if she didn't even know them? Sure, she had spoken to many people out on the streets, and dealt with plenty of customers in the shop, but they were simple patrons who made simple transactions. In the course of optimizing her ability to work in the shop she had figured out how to game smiles out of people, on occasion they told her things about their lives, and she never, ever forgot a face, but that was all part of marketing the Toy Shop, not anything meaningful. Worst of all, they must have assumed she was a heavy cyborg like Feint, not an anomalous bot. Had they known the truth, they never would have trusted her.

Would they?

She stared up after Sylvan for a long while, folding the concept repeatedly, before eventually following him upstairs.

Again, NX had to make a trip to the material manufacturer, and with the new knowledge of how far a GPS ping may or may not have traveled, she tried to make it as quick as possible. She returned with many more varieties than she had the first time. Iridescent organza, a shimmering type of twill, as close to a fully-saturated and organic satin as she could get. She stuffed her bag full with the materials that would fit, and could barely carry the rest on the bolts, but she would manage. Sylvan had plenty of ideas, written down or not, and NX had many more stashed away in her database rows for all kinds of dresses and jackets and shirts and pants for all kinds of styles of body, befitting every single type of personality profile she could work out of her emotional processing programming. Everything she conjured up internally she gave the signature line, like Sylvan said — that specific style of construction that said it came from level 3, and who, exactly, had made it.

She was eager to get back and help Sylvan make the next batch, including starting the new custom for Feint. She juggled all of the materials, dropping things only a couple of times on her way back to level 3. When she finally made it back to the shop, Sylvan was entertaining a customer.

NX hadn't considered much about it at first, but that process in the background was signaling her, like a slow, consistent pulse telling her something about the customer, and she faltered before heading into the shop, turning her primary visual arrays towards Sylvan and the customer for a closer look.

They will break him, it was saying to her, through binary ones and zeroes, electronic signals fed through her central processing unit, up to her neural synthetic interface.

She fixed her gaze on them, the way they leaned in a casual fashion onto the register counter, leering. Sylvan was a step away from the counter, a distance between that was abnormal to her. Neither of them noticed her yet, but she felt the insistent process seem to whine higher, driving the rest of her processes into a disarray.

NX thought of Sylvan's Robbie, focusing on the back of the unknown figure.

It was possible it had taken a lot of significant processing to arrive at her conclusion, but if it had, she wasn't aware of it. NX decided to go inside of the shop.

She pushed through the door, and both turned to look at her. Sylvan's expression was firm, but his eyes darted from her to the door. He was trying to tell her to turn around, and the closer she got to the stranger, the louder the complaint from her internal background processes.

Something about the crossing of their arms.

She could detect a significant emotional tenseness in the air. Sylvan wasn't breathing; he was holding his breath.

"This is my friend. She does part time work here and brings in materials," Sylvan said tightly.

The person looked at Sylvan, as if there were words to be said that couldn't be uttered in front of her.

They must have been one of the three troublesome types, and NX thought he had the same feeling as the loan agent she had seen pass overhead prior.

Perhaps it was even the same person.

NX put the fabric bolts down beside the door, along with the bag.

They took him and I did nothing, NX recalled Sylvan's voice.

"Hello! It's nice to meet you," NX said cheerily, smiling. She came forward, thrusting out her hand to shake with the stranger.

The stranger had a look of surprise in their eyes, caught off guard, but shook her hand. "Don't mind me, I'll be out of your way in a second, just putting away these materials."

The stranger said nothing, but regarded her warily after they broke hands.

NX scooped up her items and made towards the stairs, ascending.

"How do you have capital to pay someone for *work*?" The person asked Sylvan in a low hiss.

"She's just a friend of mine. I give her money for materials and she gets them for me," Sylvan said a little softly. NX kept her steps on the stairs quiet so she could continue listening. He spoke suddenly again, like he had determined something unspoken. "She has an incredible custom build for a cyborg down here, don't you think?"

Perhaps if she were not an anomalous bot, had she not already learned from Sylvan's own words, she would have bouncily corrected him. It was dangerous to have bots down in the lower levels, especially if anyone could come take them. She didn't stop ascending the stairs.

NX reached the top, and a pervasive silence struck for moments between.

"Understand why I'm here. All of a sudden you're ahead on payments. You have to know how suspicious that looks," said the person.

"I've just had a good string of sales since the last flood. It must've wiped out some competition or—"

"If you're lying to me, Mr. Hardwell..."

"Oh, come on with the '*Mister Hardwell*', Jerry."

"If I find out something you don't want me to, it will not be good for you."

"Well... What would you find out?"

"Maybe that you're bootlegging luxury top-side brands," said the voice.

Sylvan let out a strange guffaw. "I'm definitely not doing that."

"Word on the street is you're competing with Faradey."

"How could *I* compete with Faradey? Faradey is an interplanetary brand and I can't even leave my own shop."

"All I know is your work is heading top-side and if it does, people will not be happy. Things may seem like they're going good for you right now, but whatever you're up to, you need to stop it. You know me, you know I'm from these parts and I am *warning* you Sylvan, things can get a *lot* uglier for you and your *friend* very quickly."

"I'm not doing anything wrong, just trying to survive," Sylvan said, a mutter so quiet NX almost didn't detect it.

"You better be sure of that," said the voice, and NX heard footsteps, followed by the door shutting.

Then, silence.

NX peered down the stairs.

"Sylvan? Are you okay?" She called.

Sylvan let out a huff, then he appeared at the bottom of the stairs. "Yeah, I'm fine. He won't do anything. He's just trying to rattle me."

"Why would he do that? You're paying them back." NX frowned.

"The longer I owe them, the more money I have to pay. The amount I've paid over the years exceeds the value of what I have, but I've still hardly made a dent in the principal balance." Sylvan said, tipping his head up towards her. "It's better for them if I don't and I keep paying interest. And I think loan agents are sadists."

NX knew far too well in her internal knowledgebase what a sadist was.

"I was afraid they were going to hurt you," NX said. It was Sylvan's turn to furrow his brows.

"Why would you think that?"

NX shrugged. "Sometimes my programming sends me these alerts about people."

"Alerts? About what?"

Another shrug. "Like the way they might be standing, or something they say, the tone of their voice and the words they choose. I think my programming got used to identifying when there was a risk someone might break me, and eventually started to warn me if someone *seemed* dangerous. It's not always accurate, though. Like that time they had shut you off and I came in, it was trying to tell me you were dangerous, but I know you're not."

NX recalled the memory, scrubbing through the playback in her interface briefly to review it.

"That's because I was angry," Sylvan said quietly. "You knew I wanted to break *something* but thought it could've been you."

NX nodded, returning the memory to her long term memory storage.

Sylvan was silent for a long while, seeming to think on it before he put it aside, beginning up the stairs.

"Will you show me what you got?"

"Of course," NX smiled, and Sylvan arrived at the top of the stairs. NX began to spread out the bolts slightly, unraveling them, pulling things from her bag to place them out for Sylvan to assess.

He did that gesture of his, standing with his chin in his hand as his eyes worked over the materials, up and down, left and right, like he was pulling them apart internally and reorganizing them. She enjoyed watching the way he seemed to visibly compute, waiting patiently for any hint of what he was computing about.

"I think we can get quite a few more things out of this. And if Feint keeps getting more custom designs out of us, we're going to be in good shape." He said.

"What about Faradey?" NX asked.

"What about them?"

"What if it's like that person said?"

"It's not. Our designs are entirely different, we don't even use their base pattern, and we're not trying to pass it off as Faradey. Just because we made one or two pieces that bear a passing resemblance with Faradey pieces doesn't mean we're going to get in trouble with them." He said, and he sounded certain. "The loan agents will say anything to make you nervous, but we're not doing anything wrong."

"Just trying to survive," NX repeated.

"Exactly," Sylvan said, then gestured with his hand. "If you want to start on any of this, have at it. I trust you and your artistic vision. I'll watch the shop for the rest of the day."

Then he turned and went back down the stairs, leaving it to her.

00110011 00110010: 32

It was NX's turn to toil over the fabrics, the trims, the notions, putting together a pattern onto one of Sylvan's mannequins, honed into Feint's measurements, pinning and pulling and making adjustments, applying digital changes in her interface, overlaying them to make sure they visually appealed and had the correct sort of balance that the piece needed. She compared to Sylvan's sketch on occasion, and even though she was deviating from his sketch by including what Sylvan deemed as her "artistic voice" into the process, she made mostly curt, small changes that affected the symmetry, shape, and silhouette of the piece. When they were all completed, the tiny things changed the entirety, and between her construction work and Sylvan's drawing — along with the original vision from Faradey — they would have something spectacular.

Feint would be pleased, NX thought. NX was working around her shape, modifying the original design to flatter the particular angles of the custom nature of her build.

NX built the pattern in her neural synthetic interface, stashing it into her databases. She thought it was getting easier to make them, and she was not certain if it was due to her anomalous nature that she was finding such a task to be simpler to navigate over time. She was a bot, and as with any neural synthetic interface enabled bot with a gelatin suspension matrix brain, she was capable of learning. The same way her programming had recorded and then modified itself to avoid conflict with people who sent silent aggressive signals, it would fold over data in other places, too. Data would be sorted, and usually an optimization path would be determined. The neural synthetic interface preferred the pathway with least resistance in favor of optimization, and thus any bot could learn… so said NX's instruction and owner's manual, another bit of information that had been permanently inscribed into her system somewhere.

But what it didn't say was anything about if a bot were capable of creating, and if it was, if that was part of the base programming or not. Autonomous bots were capable of *doing*, but there was a difference between output and creative output, NX thought. It was the divide that separated humans and machines after all. Humanity often argued that a bot was not capable of dreaming. How could a bot create if it could not even dream?

There were differences in bot dreams and human dreams, NX certainly had learned in talking with Sylvan about it, but there was still that single dream, ever persistent.

Root.

She thought of it as she worked, ruching together tulle and lace, cutting and serging the edges of delicate flower petals, adding fine blue details to accent Feint herself. She thought of the blue sky she would see over Root, the white puffy cumulus clouds, cirrus clouds, all the different shapes of clouds across the visible spectrum of sky. That was what she was thinking as she made it, as she tucked and folded and stitched into place. If she could hold all of those clouds in her hands and shape them together, how would they look? And with what she made in fabric, how close to it would she get?

Root would have clear skies. At night, they could turn their visual arrays towards the sky and sight a straight shot towards the satellites, towards the moon, towards the offworld colonies.

She wondered what it was like to see the open sky instead of the zig-zagging metal and architectural structures she had become so accustomed to. What was it like to look up and not have an input peripheral cluttered with rails and pipes and wires and buildings? What did things look like when they were lit by the great lightbulb that was the sun?

She thought of the shimmering accents Sylvan liked to add to the pieces, and the crystalline nature of the faux opal in her synthetic skin. She would add some elements of that too, in order for it to glisten in sunlight.

What kinds of bots would she meet in such a place like that? There were many shapes, some like her, some more human, and some not human at all — like the yellow-and-black laborbot she had met on her brief encounter at the start of her fortuitous journey. She imagined them functioning under the opened sky, completing their tasks — the ones they had set for themselves.

By the time she was done daydreaming it, she had just about completed the garment, her hands working to neatly attach a few silver accent beads to the top ruching around the bust. She brushed her hands over it, tucking the fabric carefully, adjusting here and there on the mannequin, and then she turned to call for Sylvan, eager for him to see.

Circuits startled, she stepped back when she saw Sylvan was already at the top of the stairs, leaning into the doorframe, arms over his chest as he smiled, watching her.

She did not know how long he had been there, or when he had arrived. He had snuck up on her at some point during her making — during her dreaming.

"You don't even need me, do you?" He asked.

"It was your design," NX said sheepishly.

"No it wasn't," Sylvan said, making his way over. He got close, inspecting the billowy white garment with the cobalt blue thread accents, the tiny iridescent faux pearls and beads she had attached around the collar, the fade of the layers of the tulle and the purposely placed flower petals trapped between. He regarded the strands of opalescent silver that threaded almost imperceptibly through the bodice with a guided fingertip.

"What do you mean?" NX frowned, watching him work it over visually. "I followed your drawing."

Sylvan shook his head. "You took it way further than that. I added a few things to the original design, but you made this... Otherworldly."

NX could not formulate a response. Sylvan fluffed a curl of tulle and turned his head to look at her.

"What were you thinking about?" He asked.

"Root," she said. "The clouds that might be over Root."

Sylvan made a tiny noise, half a huff, a quarter of a laugh, and a quarter of a small *hmm* sound.

"I hope I get to see it someday," NX said.

"I hope you do, too," Sylvan said. "And when you do I hope you'll send me a letter."

It was NX's turn to smile. "No, silly, if I see it, then I'll bring you to see it too."

"I thought it was only bots," Sylvan reasoned. "There'd be no place for me."

"I'm sure that you would be an exception to the rule." NX answered with the same certainty Sylvan gave his designs.

Sylvan gave another small huff, relenting.

"I'll let Feint know. She loved that jacket, but she's going to be beyond thrilled with this. I hope she's got somewhere special to wear it," he said. "Someone might jump her for this one."

NX laughed. "We can't have our only repeat custom client getting hurt."

"Definitely not. We'll pack it up for her after she sees it," he said with a smirk. "Can't have her wearing this one out."

NX had not been far from Sylvan's shop, aside from her wayward visit to the materials manufacturer, but even only a floor or two up customers were on the lookout for her, and they flagged her down and flocked to her, as they normally did, when she ascended the staircase and crested the top with a satchel full of freshly crafted goods.

Sylvan was on a kick of creating accessory items out of smaller pieces of materials and scraps, trying to make the absolute most out of what NX brought back so they could maximize their revenue. He had conceptualized a lot of neckwear and hair pieces that he and NX took turns crafting throughout the night, and they took up so little space inside of the satchel that NX could carry a lot of them in the hopes of having a piece for everyone.

It was going well, NX pulling out various colored bows and ties and ascots, handing them out for people to look over. If the first person she handed it to didn't want it, they handed it to the person beside them, and then eventually the piece would find a permanent residence with someone in the crowd. The people were hungry and eager for the one-of-a-kind designs they were making, unique to level 3, not anything that was obtainable anywhere close to the surface, perhaps not anywhere on all of the surface.

That was what they started to say eventually. Who needed a Faradey or a Curie when they had bespoke works crafted right from the bowels of their own city? Beautiful and unique, just like the residents, some of them said.

The way they acted when they handled the pieces was curious. Sometimes, a customer would have such a visceral reaction to a piece that they clutched it tightly, as if frightened someone would steal it from them. *It's like it was made for me*, she heard once, twice, over and over again. What she and Sylvan made and the designs they explored together was a reflection of what they saw around them, and the residents seemed to see that too.

The statements, and the meanings behind them, filled NX with that hot-circuit warmth she had begun to associate with joy, and she pocketed them away into the parts of her database she meant to keep forever, beside Sylvan and the shop and the yellow-and-black laborbot that had showed her that tiny bit of kindness in the beginning, and all those trace data fragments she held dear.

She had gotten about halfway through her stock of pieces when the small crowd that had amassed suddenly began to stir uncomfortably. They looked down at their hands, their wrists, murmurs starting to rumble through the group, and NX saw the darting glances indicative of panic bubbling amongst them. When they got stirred up, she did too, and she listened.

"What's happening?" She asked.

"There's return agents heading down towards the lower levels," one of them said. "They're on level 5 and they brought PTX muscle with them."

Sylvan had said they were mercenaries, and the worst of the bunch. Hired cybernetic hands to recover assets.

They must have been coming for her.

A couple of people peeled away from the crowd, swiftly making themselves scarce within the level's architecture. NX gaped, feeling her rows beginning to freeze up. She zipped up her satchel pointedly.

Suddenly, an arm grabbed hers.

NX felt her system stifle a scream.

She had been too careless, walking amongst them like that. Sylvan had warned her enough times not to mention or show she was ano, that they might want to cannibalize her parts, that they'd do anything to scrape together a few chips to get ahead on their collective debt. She would be powerless to do anything to resist. She was just a personal model, she was—

"Doll, we've gotta hide you," said the resident, hand clasped on her arm, a man with green eyes and black lips and tightly curled locs on his head. Nods went through the rest of the crowd, faces turned towards her, determination in their eyes. He gave her a soft pull, and the bodies parted. The seizure in her processes began to slowly release as she followed, the crowd falling in line behind them.

They knew she was a bot — an anomalous bot — and they didn't care.

It was like Sylvan said.

She was one of them.

The small group ushered her across the way, down a half of a level, through a tight squeeze of an alley, twisting her through a less-traveled area she had never explored before. At the end, an opened door awaited, a shadow holding it ajar as warm dim yellow lighting invited them inside. The green-eyed man led the way, and the mass of them filed through the door, the last person tucking it shut behind them.

All of the word-of-mouth, the wayward conversations she had in the shop, the way she knew their names when they gave them, and their emotional states, how she knew each and every one of those faces that clustered about her, ushering her through the door, it all meant something to them, something much more than she had initially believed. She had thought they were just customers, people who wanted something and didn't really care where it came from, but she could see, glistening like a gem amidst slag, what Sylvan had, and why he had felt so loyal to them.

It wasn't Root, and they weren't bots, but it was difficult for her to process the consideration that Root would have been much different.

"They won't find you in here," said one of the people that had piled in behind her. Another round of nods went through the small clutch of them as they wound through a hallway, led by the green-eyed man. He brought them to an opening of a shared space, where people paused what they were doing and craned to see her.

"Is that her?" A voice asked from somewhere in the corner.

When the green-eyed man finally stopped and let her go, her entourage started to chatter quiet conversation amongst themselves. She could hear them mentioning Sylvan's name, in parts, checking their devices connected to the human internet as they calculated something unknowable to her. A few more people gathered into the room, standing in doorways and the hall, eyes turned towards her.

Finally, a voice spoke up:

"Can we see what else you have?"

NX smiled and unzipped her satchel.

The residents that had hidden her told Sylvan over the human internet that NX was there with them and safe, so he didn't worry about her when she didn't return right away.

NX felt grateful for such a simple action. She did not want Sylvan to fret over her, and she certainly did not want him to lapse away in that fretfulness. He was on a trajectory upwards, and NX would have been disappointed if something so silly as herself would disrupt that.

She had returned sometime late at night, when Sylvan was supposed to have turned off the shop's lights so people didn't think he was still open. The lights still blared from the interior, bathing everything around it in the familiar greenish glow, and Sylvan was by the register, head down as he sometimes got when he was fighting off sleep. She pushed through the door, and Sylvan's head snapped up to alertness.

NX turned and locked the door behind her.

They didn't talk after that.

The NX of weeks ago may have quantified that as strange, but at that moment, she didn't. The silence that prevailed between her and Sylvan seemed to deliver yottabytes of data all on its own. NX had narrowly avoided the return agents, which could or could not have been there specifically to return her, but the danger, previously some far and away idea, was nearly knocking on the front door of the shop.

Both of them knew NX could not duck and dodge them forever, with or without the help of the level 3 denizens, and it seemed impossible to generate any sort of plan for when the eventuality would come that NX would not come back to the shop.

Neither she nor Sylvan wanted to audibly speak about it, because it made it all the more tangible.

NX did not close her eyes when she rested on her charger that night, sitting with her knees to her chest and her arms over them, staring into the floorboards of the living quarters. She had not entered into full standby, so charging was sluggish, but still on the uptick. Sylvan would steal a glance at her, unable to rest either.

Finally, at an early hour, Sylvan opened his mouth to speak, and NX cut him off.

"I'm not leaving," she insisted.

Sylvan didn't let a vowel escape his lips. He just shut his mouth and looked at her.

The GPS pings wouldn't make it through.

The people *wanted* her there, and she wanted to be there with them.

They had Feint's order ready, a pile of new pieces Sylvan had poured all his nervousness into while she was away, and a looming unspoken and piled potential that seemed to stuff so tightly into the room it was hard to move through.

Level 3 was safe.

It had to be.

—

NX stuck to the shop that next day.

Sylvan had floated the idea of staying closed and working upstairs, if they had to do anything at all. NX did not think he had slept at all, and NX had only managed to a 75% charge herself, not topped up as much as she would have liked. Still, she knew it was important to keep carrying on and not dash any of the progress they had made, so she had insisted that they open.

Besides, Feint was supposed to be coming to retrieve her dress, and NX so desperately wanted to save the look on her face when she saw it.

It was about halfway through the workday when a large gray and black bot stopped outside of the door, standing beside it.

Curious, NX strained to make out the details of the bot through the panes of the windows and doors; she could not calculate much of it other than it was tall, imposing, and black and grey. Its feet were heavy on the metal grating of the gangplank outside.

"Oh, shit," Sylvan uttered, knowing something she didn't, and she looked to him: 90% fear. He grabbed NX and pushed her behind him wordlessly.

Two nearly identical pale-faced, suavely black-suited men swiftly pushed through the door. They were too smartly dressed to be from the lower levels, and NX thought the bot they brought with them appeared too imposing and expensive to be from any of the mid-levels.

The suited men approached, stopping a meter or two from Sylvan.

"Mr. Hardwell, we have reason to believe an unauthorized autonomous android is situated on this premises," one said flatly.

"An unauthorized android?" Sylvan repeated.

"Global positioning satellite pinpoints a custom NX1000 model in this vicinity, serial number NXVTY2619402," said the other. He held up his palm towards Sylvan to show him something. NX did not dare try to strain around Sylvan to see. "The android is property of Showcase Enterprises and is believed to have been misplaced."

Her original owners. They were return agents, come to collect. Not good.

Sylvan took a tiny step backwards, brushing into NX. Covertly, he reached behind, grabbed at the cloth on her stomach, and gave it a squeeze. He was trying to tell her something, and she was not certain what it was.

"Your pings must be wrong. Signals get messed up all the time down here. It's possible—" Sylvan started.

"You do know the penalty for failure to return a claimed android is a fine and jail time, correct?" The first one broke in.

"Failure to return a claimed android for thirty days upgrades the offense to theft of services as well as grand larceny for the pro-rated cost of the machine," finished the other.

"I didn't steal anything," Sylvan said. "No one is doing anything wrong."

"Turn over the machine so we may return it to its owners," said one of the men.

To her *owners*. She had come so far from those terrible nightly flashes and the order of work she was expected to conduct. She had saved so many memories, and she had aligned her ownership to Sylvan, only because she had *wanted* to. She had done so much, had assisted, had really made a difference, and she had learned, understood, and *grown*, she thought. She had created and she had dreamed and she had a *soul*.

She couldn't go back.

She couldn't stand in line, naked and memoryless, awaiting the next client to break her to pieces, scrounging up scraps of ghost data in the hopes it meant something more.

"No," NX heard herself whisper.

Sylvan squeezed on her shirt again, and she understood what he was saying.

He was telling her to run.

NX aligned her processes as best as she could, and then she darted right, dashing about the register counter, pushing over a rack into one of the men. He was knocked over by the sudden avalanche of product and the rack itself, but the other man saw her, and he grabbed her with a swift fist in a knot of the back of her shirt.

"No!" NX squealed. "I won't go! I won't go back!"

"Let her go!" Sylvan howled.

Sylvan hurled himself forward, throwing his hard metal shoulder into the man who had grabbed NX's shirt. The man didn't let go, but the shirt tore, and NX stumbled towards the door. Sylvan wrapped his arms around the man, containing him, but the other man that had been knocked down bounced to his feet, grabbing NX by the wrist before she could reach the pushbar on the door.

NX wrenched on her arm, tried to pull away, but the man was strong, far stronger than her.

"Sylvan!" NX screamed. "Sylvan, you can't let them take me back! I can't go back!"

And far stronger than Sylvan, too.

He had used all of the strength in his metallic arms to pin the second man down, but the second man flexed through him, denting and fracturing his cybernetics like they were simply made of brittle plastic. Sylvan's joints popped, spurting small sparks as the wiring shorted and the man broke free.

Sylvan was just as powerless to those men as she was.

"Resist and I will damage you," the man holding NX's arm hissed.

She didn't want to be broken.

Or disassembled.

But she wanted even less to go back, to be broken and disassembled over and over again and never even know.

"Let her *go*!" Sylvan yelled, charging the men at the door again, broken or not. The other man moved into his way and swung a fist at him, connecting so quickly he dropped Sylvan to the ground faster than NX knew it was happening.

"Sylvan!" NX cried, turning to see the red of his organic blood staining his motionless face, trailing from his nose, his body sprawled along the shop floor.

The man tightened his grip on NX's wrist.

"Disable it," the other man said.

"No!" NX yelled.

Someone put a hand on the back of her neck, forcing her down towards the ground, searching out her direct neural synthetic access ports.

They will break you, she thought, and she knew it was true. They would break her. They would do much worse than that.

NX grit her teeth together in a hard clench, and decided that if she had to break herself to get away from them, she would.

It was easier than she thought.

With a twist, an incessant, annoying alert that she was causing damage to herself, a howl in her interface that was meant to mimic pain in some way, the mechanical parts of her elbow joint tore under the stress, the piece of her frame going with it, along with the synthetic muscles and skin, and she was suddenly and abruptly free.

She could disappear into the lower levels, hide amidst the customers that knew her, the connections she had forged, and they would believe she had been smothered beneath the next flood, her electronics and circuitry waterlogged and destroyed forever.

She heard the men clambering behind her.

NX leapt for the door, slamming it open.

And as she thought she was mere steps from freedom, she ran clear into the massive grey and black bot, suddenly before her, standing like an unmoving monolith. Unceremoniously, it reached down to grab her with claw-like hands, pinching on her synthetic skin, cutting through it to her metal chassis beneath, lifting her into the air. The bot stared at her blankly with blue flickering eyes, solid, unfeeling, and unthinking. She screamed, but the bot was impervious, faltering not in the faintest degree, its solid metal and plastic parts as firm and unrelenting as the architecture around her.

"Good, PTX," one of the men said, emerging behind her.

The second man threw NX's severed arm over the rail of the catwalk.

"Return," the man ordered the bot, and with NX held firm in its grip, it began to walk in front of the two men, retreating in some unknowable direction.

NX struggled, but her synthetic body was weak against the hulking mechanical nature of the bot that held her, its feet stomping a metallic jangle as it plodded, one foot, then the next, making its way to the stairs. NX let out an audible screech, her vocal synthesizer screaming in pitches she didn't know she was capable of making, but there was no one, not a single human or cyborg, available to hear her.

Her cries echoed through the buildings.

The party of three plus NX made it to the next floor up, the two men moving in front of the bot confining her as they went, pulling up the lead. As they made it towards the next floor, they abruptly stopped on the stairs.

"Put her down, *now*," a familiar feminine voice said.

Feint! Coming to get her garment.

"Miss Faradey, what are you doing down here?" One of the men asked.

Miss Faradey?

NX could not see beyond the bot that held her.

"That is a command, bot. Invocation of law five. Put her *down*." Feint's voice said. The bot holding NX complied like it was unable to resist, placing NX down onto the grating of the gangplank. NX felt her body sway, cut and sliced and crushed and damaged, errors flashing in her interface as she scrambled to reconfigure a few things to remain standing.

NX spared a shaky glance back to see Feint, surrounded by her own entourage of blank grey securitybots, three bringing up her rear and tightening behind her, as if waiting for an order from her to intervene.

NX's processes swirled, incessant, blinking, confused.

"We are under law three jurisdiction, which supersedes law five, especially in regards to ownership," said one of the men that had tried to take her, but NX didn't give any more pause in cycles to let him say more. She squeezed behind the massive bot and past the reach of the two men.

"Hey!" One of them called after her.

NX looked back for a brief moment to see the familiar woman, the white ethereal cyborg woman that had requested the Faradey jacket clone in white, the repeat customer, Feint, watching her slip away, a firm expression on her face. She made a gesture with her hand, and the grey bots tangled themselves up in the PTX and the return agents. NX heard the metal of the streets groan under their combined weight as they clashed.

Miss Faradey, the man had called her, and NX's data spiraled. Feint Faradey.

She had tried to buy NX some time.

One of the men howled, and the huge PTX bot started to fight free of the grey securitybots. It was only a matter of time before it or the return agents broke free. She didn't give any pause to look back again, and she hurled herself around the catwalks.

She circled higher, towards level 6, passing through clusters of cyborgs and bots flitting through the air. She recognized the faces, the shocked look of customers, wearing *their* apparel, as she pushed past them. At first, some of them just stared, open-mouthed and wide eyed, unsure what to do, and then, when she peered back, she saw them close ranks behind her.

They were helping her.

They were slowing them down, and she could see it if she looked behind her, loping fast as she was, using every digit of her battery power to try to make an escape.

The knowledge reinvigorated her, and she felt full in her chest, complete in the data that filled her database rows. Those men wouldn't stop, and they'd hurt those people who were obstructing their way, but just the fact that the denizens had done that *for her* was enough to bring a grateful smile to her face, despite the heavy grip of fear hot on her heels.

Maybe, if she was lucky, she would escape. Maybe there was a slim chance of it.

When the denizens wouldn't stop getting in their way, the men, with their athletic build cybernetics, jumped and spidered across the walls instead, and NX felt her luck dashing in real time.

NX surged onward.

She twisted a corner onto level 9 and one of the men popped up over the rail, heading her off, and she backed.

The other man came at her back, slamming through the metal grated flooring, and NX had nowhere to go.

Except on the rail.

NX, with her remaining hand, grabbed the rail and hurled herself over, tumbling over herself as she careened downwards.

Maybe falling would be her last memory, too.

She did not know how many levels carried the city down, but she knew that down there was anything better than what awaited her above.

NX let herself fall.

But that time there was no stroke of luck to stop her.

00110011 00110101: 35

NX's startup sequence began some unknown amount of cycles later.

~~For a long while, her processes were dark. She was not in~~ control of her limbs, and her internal diagnostics screamed, blinking and flashing and exclaiming about all of the things that were broken, and all of the things that were missing. Data was corrupted, digits and artifacts crawling across her interfacing. Her bot net connection was entirely severed, and data backed up backed up backed backed up in her system.

Everything everything repeated repeated , some semblance of broken.

A missing arm, a missing eye, a broken networking component, and so many more parts, an impossibly long list of parts that were disconnected, missing, or nonfunctional. Her non-functioning olfactory sensors were activated then, haywire as they informed her of the incessantly offensive odor everywhere around her.

It was slow and gradual, but eventually, she regained control of her limbs.

She was face down in a mound of something, and she gave a push push with her remaining arm.

~~Pieces fell off of her back, but her visual array was still~~ somewhat functional. The data that it gave her led her to infer her location.

A sky, of sorts.

A drone whizzed overhead and NX held still.

When her cracked audio ~~sensors did not detect the drone any~~ longer, she pushed again, managing to sit up. Many of her actuators

actuators were damaged, but she assessed herself visually as best as she could, looking over the torn synthetic skin, missing from her chest and torso, exposing her chassis paneling, silver in color, and wiring, looped and looped and looped, falling out of her like the knotted curl of a tangled bobbin.

NX set her remaining visual array on what was around her.

Sylvan had taught her how to make use of things, how to create, how to repair. She may have been in a landfill, stockpiled with broken, disheveled, destroyed machines, but there must have been some components she could use. She was happyhappy that her memories, despite the damage to her systems that caused glitches and hiccups, still seemed to be intact. Her body could be repaired, but the memories would have been gone forever. With some effort and reconfiguring of the background programming she used to gain balance, she got to her feet and began searching, scanning her visual array along the detritus around her.

She had not loped far before reaching what appeared to be a promising pile of smaller components — wires and circuits — and she dropped to her knees, then used her remaining arm to begin to dig into it. In that pile, it was possible she could find a new eye, or at least parts of an eye she could use to start beginning a repair that would eventually become part of her visual sensory array.

Without two eyes — really the only parts of a visual array that a personal model bot like NX had — meant her visibility was down by 50%, and she did not see the other bot until it was almost on top of her.

A bright yellowyellow bot, fully functional, standing to the side of her, cyan ring light eyes regarding her.

She thought instantly of the bot, the big gray one that had grabbed her, crushed her, had not responded to her screams.

No, it wasn't the same bot. The laborbot before her was large, but not the same kind of bot as the gray one. They weren't even the same color.

It was more like...

Bots didn't have the same emotional determinations on their faces, and NX was unable to read anything when she applied her emotional ~~processing algorithms to the yellow-and-black bot's~~ silicone face plates. She may as well have been trying to determine emotional complexities from Sylvan's sewingsewing machine.

She fell into default. The bot was likely there to protect the parts dumped into the landfill. NX was not supposed to be active, ~~nor pawing through the parts.~~

"I'm sorry, I'll go, I won't cause any trouble..." She said, getting slowly to her feet. She braced to run, but she doubted she could get far from an obviously undamaged bot.

"Wait, don't go yet. What are you looking for?" The bot asked, not stern, but oddly calm.

Another ano bot? She considered. Perhaps it was possible that she was not the only bot to awaken in the landfill, not the only one to be dumped amongst the piles of trash. NX had been lucky up until that final day, and she clung to the idea idea that she was still lucky, that she had not only survived and restarted there, but she came back to activity at just the right time, at the exact moment to cross paths with a sympathetic laborbot.

Another sympathetic laborbot, she recalled. How luckycky she was to find *two* of them. Her luck had *not* yet run out.

"I..." NX stuttered uncontrollably. "I was looking for a replacement eye."

The laborbot scanned her.

"What's your model?" The bot asked.

~~"NX." She said cautiously.~~

"I know where one is," the bot said, and then to her surprise, the bot smiled.

01000101 01110000 01101001 01101100 01101111 01100111 01110101 01100101: EPILOGUE

NX — renamed, appropriately, Inix with the help of her new-yet-old friend laborbot Sterling — had not gotten a chance to find out if Sylvan was okay after their altercation with the return agents, but with a little help from her new mysterious militarybot friend Zev, she heard he was.

Inix was so lucky to have met them. In fact, she had re-met them, the same two bots she had come into contact with on her first leap of faith into the city's levels. Both of them had helped to repair her and commenced upon their own journey before eventually returning to their home and safe space at the landfill. Sterling, the kindly laborbot, and Zev, the unexplainable undetectable force that had driven her away in an effort to protect Sterling. She was a danger to them back then, Zev explained, with her degrading lithium ion battery and her GPS chip. Zev had disabled the locational chip and promised he would assist her with a power upgrade of sorts to make her more independent.

More free.

She thought often of Sylvan as she spent time amongst the other bots, about the gift the two bots have given her in bringing her and Sylvan together. She treasured those memories deeply, but she knew she was not able to let everything stay as it was, permanently there with them amidst the trash in the junkyard. Most of all, she wanted to thank Sylvan, for everything he did and tried to do for her.

She knew of one surefire way to thank him properly.

It took some time to prepare as Zev and Sterling had returned from their adventure damaged, but eventually, and with little fanfare, Sterling and Zev came alongside her into the city, down to level 3, following the breadcrumb memory path Inix had saved.

Zev was fearless, and Inix attributed much of that to his make as a militarybot. Inix, though, felt her circuits freeze up with anxiousness. She did not know what to expect when she reached Sylvan. He had been pretty damaged last she had seen him, and he wasn't in any shape financially to get repaired or to replace his cybernetics. Sterling, sweet laborbot that he was, consoled her gently; if he hadn't been such a big bot, and she hadn't experienced his robotic body prior to his personalized customizations with stolen synthetic skin, she would have sworn he was a human-based cyborg.

Zev was sweet too, but his kindness was much more nuanced.

He was, after all, the one that had saved her — and driven her off, all within cycles of each other.

Their small trio entourage made through the levels until Inix caught sight of the shop, familiar to her databases, and she smiled at the warm glow of the lights inside. From a distance, she saw Sylvan leaned over his register counter, working on something. Probably drawing, she thought. He looked deep in consideration, brows furrowed, and she watched him silently from afar, holding the moments dear.

He looked broken, his cybernetics cracked and scuffed, and Inix's smile faltered.

"Go ahead," Sterling urged. "He's waiting for you."

Inix started forward, suddenly aware of what she was wearing. Sylvan would judge it, of course, but it was something to make her less apparent, something she had bartered for, little more than dredges half scraped from the landfill. Sterling had given her some gold he had collected from discarded circuit boards in the landfill, and with a tiny nugget of it, she had traded for a decent jacket on the outskirts of the city.

She pushed open the shop door, OPEN illuminated in the pane.

Sylvan glanced up, for just a second, then glanced away.

Then he looked again, and he smiled.

"*Honey*, no way!" He exclaimed, and he rushed around the register counter.

"Sylvan," Inix grinned. He came towards her quickly, ghost data telling her to step backwards, that he would break her, but she overrode it, all of it, knowing Sylvan never would. He wrapped his arms around her in a hug, not very tight, but enough that she felt it.

She embraced him in return, pushing her black opal silicone fingers into his back, shifting up onto her toes to lean into him.

"I can't believe you..." he started, letting go of her and stepping back, then he regarded her with a small sneer of disgust. "Honey, what are you *wearing*?"

Inix laughed. "It's Inix, now. And I knew you were going to say that."

"Inix," he repeated. "Fitting."

Behind her, Sterling ducked in through the doorframe, and Sylvan's eyes widened at the bot's large presence.

"Sylvan, this is my friend Sterling," Inix said, gesturing for Sterling to come closer. Sterling did, albeit carefully around the racks and products, and the two of them shook hands — Sterling delicately. Inix regarded Sylvan's crushed and broken cybernetic arms and hands, quivering even with the small motion. Inix frowned, the memory of the last she had seen of him, shattered on the floor, briefly flickering through her active pathways. "You're broken."

Sylvan's smile faltered. 75% sadness. "I can't afford repairs, not that anyone would come to do them. It's not like I can—"

"There is an electro-interference frequency perimeter around your establishment. Why?" Came Zev's unmistakable voice, that tinny, raspy robotic chime he had, standing in the doorway.

Sylvan looked up, meeting Zev's bright cyan ring-light eyes in the shadowed doorway. Unlike Sterling's blue human-like eyes, Zev had kept his robot eyes. He opened his mouth to speak, but Zev vocalized before he could.

"I have disabled it, it is unnecessary." Zev said, stepping forward. Inix laughed, Sylvan's jaw nearly hit the floor.

"This is my friend Zev," Inix said with a grin. Sylvan looked at her, awed. She let out a tiny chortle, then covered her lips. "He is very, very clever. I brought him in hopes that I could repay you a little."

Sylvan managed to regain his composure, and he put out his twitching, glitching hand to shake with Zev's.

Zev just looked at it.

"Your articulation motors are damaged," Zev said. "Model type GYT4355 is obsolete, but compatible with models GYT4360, GYT4365, GYT4370, and GYT4375. Parts also from autonomous bot models TU7730, TU7740, and TU7750 are hot-swappable for your particular necessities. Replacement components may also offer significant articulation upgrades and smoother movement."

Zev paused, hardly a cycle, then said: "I have located applicable components. Would you like a repair and upgrade?"

Sylvan looked to Sterling, then to Inix. "I can't afford to purchase new components. They added the purchase price of your model to my debt and I—"

"Your debt is repaid." Zev interrupted.

"What?" Sylvan looked at him strangely.

"Your debt is repaid." Zev repeated.

Sylvan pushed his way around the register counter, toying with the register machine until he pulled up something, no doubt a confirmation of what Zev was telling him, and he staggered backwards a step. He put a hand to his head, trembling.

"Sylvan, are you okay?" Inix asked, and Sylvan nodded.

"This has to be a dream," he said.

"It's not," Sterling piped up, a small smile on his face.

"How... How could you, could anyone have done that?" Sylvan asked, shooting a glance in Zev's direction.

It was simple, Inix had learned. Though she had spent time making Sylvan's problems her own there in the shop, for a skilled and clever bot, a human's problems were easy to solve. It was, in fact, that easy for an overpowered virtual intelligence to solve it.

Inix liked to daydream about what they could have all accomplished together.

"Data manipulation." Zev said simply.

Sylvan sharply looked back to Inix, and Zev asked again:

"Would you like a repair and upgrade?"

"Inix," Sylvan asked, a forced sort of apprehension in his tone as he broke a small smile. "What kind of bots have you brought to my shop?"

SYLVAN WILL RETURN IN
The GONE Machine

GYT4355 QUICK START GUIDE

Thank you for your purchase of cybernetic enhancement limbs, model GYT. This quick start guide should help assist you in the basic operation and understanding of your new cybernetic limbs. Whether this is your first cybernetic enhancement or your fifth, we advise you to review the materials listed below and consult with the included manual to ensure optimal operation of your cybernetics.

This quick start guide covers models:

- GYT4355
- GYT4360
- GYT4365

If your model is not listed, please consult Cyberdynelife for a replacement quick start guide and manual.

STOP! Do not proceed if you have not undergone surgical implementation of cybernetic sockets and neural grafting. Please do not attempt to utilize cybernetic enhancements while disconnected from a body. "Dry" use may result in suboptimal operation up to and including irreparable damage not covered by your one year limited warranty. For more warranty information, please consult your owner's manual.

AFTER SURGICAL IMPLEMENTATION

We know you're excited to give your cybernetic enhancement limbs a whirl! Please ensure all measured testing responses are within the normal operational parameters. Your post-operational team should conduct the following analysis:

- Flex and rotational evaluation
- Hand-eye calibration
- Neural feedback load evaluation

After all tests have been passed, you're ready to experience all of the amazing things Cyberdynelife GYT model cybernetic enhancements have to offer. Comparatively to former models GYT4200, you will enjoy:

- Increased durability and operational life
- Increased stability
- Increased speed
- Increased feedback response

Manual No. 54786 (Rev. 12)

GETTING STARTED

STEP 1
ENSURE OPTIMAL CHARGE

Cyberdynelife GYT model cybernetic enhancements utilize organic energy reserves, but for first time users, this may not be enough. You may charge utilizing the sockets on the wrist, or purchase Cybernetic Enhancement Nutrient Supplements (CENS) - they're delicious and nutritious!

STEP 2
TOGGLE FUNCTIONALITY

Cyberdynelife GYT model cybernetic enhancements enjoy automatic functionality switching including sport mode, energy saver mode, and low activity mode. Selections can be made in your internal interface or using the manual toggle beneath the charging port.

STEP 3
ROUTINE MAINTENANCE

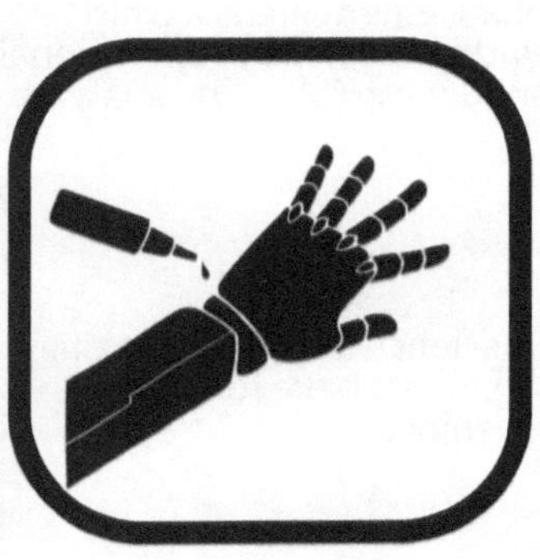

To keep your enhanced cybernetics functional, complete routine maintenance cycles. You can find details about cleaning, lubricating, and storing your cybernetics in your owner's manual.

Stop by a Cyberdynelife designated repair facility for your first FREE* tune up!

USING YOUR CYBERNETICS

Your cybernetics should require minimal training and rehabilitation. Soon, your cybernetic enhancements will become second-nature to you. Many customers report feeling like they were born with their cybernetics! Here are some ways you can begin to experience all your cybernetics have to offer:

LIFTING HEAVY OBJECTS

With increases in muscular ability delivered via pressurized synthetics, you will enjoy lifting objects you may have not been capable of lifting with organic arms or legs. In fact, Cyberdynelife model GYT cybernetics boast a 125% increase over average organic muscular strength.

CONDUCTING FINE DETAILS

Your cybernetics are capable of handling even the most delicate of tasks! Human surgeons around the world trust Cyberdynelife's cybernetic enhancements to deliver precise hands-on movements — up to an accuracy rate of 98.66%*! Cyberdynelife GYT model cybernetic enhancements are perfect for every task including skills that require accuracy — like handwriting.

CAREFUL & DELICATE

While Cyberdynelife GYT models boast increases in lifting capacity and fine motor accuracy, Cyberdynelife GYT models are also capable of handling delicate and fragile items. Collision systems, neural pressure points, and built in sensors allow touch and grip on brittle items. No more worries about bruising or tearing even the thinnest of skin! Our GYT models can hold even a butterfly.

LIGHTWEIGHT & DISCRETE

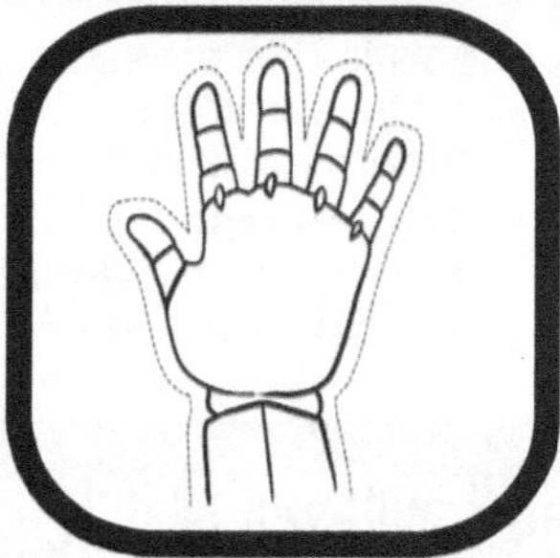

All models of Cyberdynelife GYT cybernetic enhancements are built with the same aluminum blend used in airships. Lightweight and durable, this proprietary aluminum blend won't feel like a drag. GYT models GYT4360 and GYT4365 allow for optional integration with synthetic skin, and support the use of a nanoskin module (not included).

WARNINGS

How you utilize your cybernetic enhancement limbs is ultimately up to you, but not all uses are covered under Cyberdynelife's limited one-year warranty. Some scenarios may cause damage to your cybernetic enhancement limbs.

DO NOT:

- Operate cybernetic limbs detached from an anchor point ("dry" operation)
- Operate cybernetic limbs above or below their operational temperature range (see owner's manual for details)
- Mix brand cybernetic enhancements
- Attempt to jailbreak Cyberdynelife software or firmware; doing so voids all warranties
- Attempt disassembly for purpose of repair or replacement; only Cyberdynelife certified repair technicians should repair Cyberdynelife brand cybernetic enhancements. Unauthorized repairs voids all warranties
- Submerge cybernetic enhancements unless waterproofed by an authorized Cyberdynelife certified technician

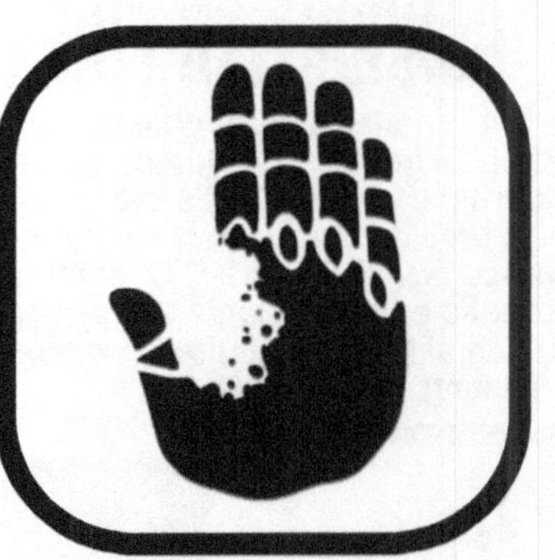

CAUTION:

- Ball joints uncovered by nanoskin or synthetic skin can snag or pinch; ensure all joints are free from obstruction at all times
- Some neural conductors may cause erratic grip pressure. Ensure the latest hardware and firmware for optimal cybernetic enhancement operation
- Keep cybernetic enhancements oiled and dry; humid and/or moist conditions can cause rusting or erratic operation

CYBER**DYNELIFE**

ACKNOWLEDGEMENTS

Can't believe it. I'm here again, with another book. No less, this was a book that you, the readers, requested. That's right - I didn't really plan to write another book full of bots after *The Warm Machine*, but I kept getting feedback saying "I wish I knew more about Inix" and "I really want to see Inix." Here she is, my beautiful bot girl Inix, in all of her glory.

I had envisioned for her something already off of the back of *The Warm Machine*, but nothing this complete. So, when people started remarking about her, I went at it on the page. I had wanted to see what city life was like, since we spent so much time outside of it, in construction zones and military bases (and of course, the landfill) in *The Warm Machine*. We got to see the cyborg gang on level one, but aside from that, it was previously just conjecture as we pass through.

The levels of the city are loosely based on the Kowloon Walled City, a structure that existed in Hong Kong up until it was demolished completely in 1993/1994. The walled city was densely populated, cheap to live in, and had a lot of crime (it was noted it was "lawless"), but a lot of the people who used to live there think of it fondly — tight knit, neighborly, and community-oriented despite residents often being quite poor. Most notably, the structure of the walled city meant living inside of it was quite dark, with no ability for sunlight to pass through. The city in *The Lucky Machine* is not at all dissimilar, except only for most of the levels existing underground and top-side residents enjoying the "luxury" of sunlight. Plus our lovely sewage floods, of course.

I hope you didn't mind the cyborgs and their role in this story. One recurring note was that people enjoyed how focused on the bots I was in the first book, but since humanity exists around them, it would not be possible for me to continue writing different types of stories and entirely ignore the human element. Sylvan seems like a good enough human, though, and through him I got to showcase how human problems and bot problems are distinctly different — and with a little bit of teamwork between humans and (rogue) bots, nothing is unachievable. Fingers crossed he's not too in the way!

Now is where I take the time to thank all of you for supporting me on this journey, listening to my whining and complaining (and infodumping), and helping me get to the final stretch, including all my writer friends, and my significant other Patrick for being the first to read it. Thank you, of course, to my editor, Amanda Silva. Special thanks to my beta readers who helped me with this lovely book! Shoutout, in no particular order: Tory Keith, N Soleil, Hayden, Jordan Stinson, PupAndPony, Steve Haley, and Kenny Farrell. Thank you to all of the amazing backers that continue to support my books and come back for more.

As always, I welcome you to tell me your thoughts and opinions, wax poetic about the characters or the setting, and everything in between. I love hearing from you, so don't be shy to reach out.

It's my sincerest hope that you enjoyed this book as much as I enjoyed writing it and... Well, I can't exactly stop on just two books, can I? Who knows what the next one might bring. ;)

PLEASE TAKE A MOMENT TO REVIEW!

Thank you so much for taking the time to read The Lucky Machine! I hope you enjoyed the story. Indie authors like me can use your support. Leaving a review can help others find good or even great books to read, will prioritize a book in certain algorithms, and generally can help your indie author feel good about their offering to the world. Want to help by leaving a review? Please leave me a review on Amazon, GoodReads, The Storygraph, or your favorite place to leave book reviews!